MW01172148

IN HIS WIND

By Rev. Al Paquette

Travel through the life of a man who chooses to spend his time behind bars

www hd4jc.com

ISBN 978-1-4499740-8-4

Printed in the USA

Written by Al Paquette, with the help of John Emiba

Cover Design By Al Paquette

Cover photographs By Dave Dillman

Book formatted by Bill Alderman

www.oltermann@hotmail.com

ACKNOWLEDGMENTS

I would like to thank all the hard workers behind the scenes. All the folks that I take for granted who have worked hard to plan the prison invasions and paved the way for our ministry.

Thank you to:

God for His unconditional love.

Jesus for walking with me every day.

My mom who has always been there for me and still encourages me.

Barry and Lynda who encouraged me to write this book.

Lynda who had to interpret my gangster accent onto paper and Barry for designing our logo and the many hours he has spent on all of the projects to help our ministry.

Dutch who has allowed me to print our APM newsletter.

Brian for the many hours he spent on the DOIN TIME chopper.

All our faithful supporters that believe in the vision God gave us.

The chaplains for allowing us to be their guest.

The prison officials and staff who have to work extra hard when we come into their prisons.

All the people that I have not mentioned, if you know me you know that I love you all.

FOREWORD

COMMENTS FROM INMATES

One of the ways Al has helped me is his consistency of bringing the love of Christ to us and sharing in our suffering! This is very powerful as the majority of society continues to hate and ridicule those that are incarcerated. Al meets us where we are just as Jesus met the two thieves at Calvary while hanging on the cross!

Tiny

I'm thankful for the Lord for sending Al into my life and sharing the word with me. The Lord has helped me through all the years that I have been on death row and the gift He gave me to help me with my time here. He gave me a new peace within, to go through all I put on myself and only He can work it out for His glory.

Paul

After meeting Al, my life in prison took on a whole new meaning. It brought release and relief from the bondage of being incarcerated. I found new gifts from within that I am now able to share with others. I never knew that I could sing a little until I got with the Palanka Players. I now have a positive outlook on my life.

Eugene

Al's life with Sharon and our Lord is an inspiration to many and I trust this book will touch many lives for Jesus.

Dave

While I was incarcerated in Florida I was a homosexual. I used to steal, fight, curse and whatever else you can think of. I used to go to church playing like I had Jesus. But I really went to see my so called friends. I went one Tues. night to church and this man, Mr. Al, stepped up on the platform and spoke. Who knew that that night was going to be part of my life changing. His words were so touching and real. The reason I listened to him is that I like bikes and tattoos and he had both of them. He told us to give God a chance. When I went back to the dorm later that night I prayed and felt different.

John

1

You know you are truly Scooter Trash if
you ride for the enjoyment, not the status.
Jun 7, Scooter Trash Calendar

My mother once told me that my first few days on this earth were almost my last.

A terrible gloom had crept up on New England like a thief in the night. The streetlights barely shone through the gusts of a snowstorm making the usually soft particles seem like shards of glass blasting through. A young woman with a small but sturdy build pushed through the turbulence with a little bundle pressed against her chest. The head nurse pleaded with the woman to stay, but to no avail. Just when she thought it could get no worse, a violent rush of wind came at her with such an impact that all she could do was to stay idle as if pushing a brick wall. An upward draft came up and nearly snatched the package out of her arms. With a panicked motion, she managed to keep the contents inside the warmth of the blanket. As the wind subsided a little, she peeled back a corner of the blanket to reveal a hardy three-day-old baby boy with a smile that said he was unaware of the danger he had just faced. Little did I realize that this was the start, a sign from heaven, of the rocky road that lay ahead.

If I had a chance to live my life all over again, I would not change any of it. I only regret hurting the people I love most. However, I am thankful for my past because it is what makes me the person that I am today. The pain I caused, the property I destroyed, and the drugs I ingested were all part of God's plan. I am living proof of God's love and the ability to overcome all odds through Him and His will.

I have always described myself as being a bad kid. I am not a bad person by nature, but when I was young I had to work hard to be bad. With the aid of drugs later on, this came natural. The more drugs I did the more bad choices I made.

My grandfather came from Canada many years ago to start Slade Laundry, named after Slade Street, in Fall River, Massachusetts. My dad and his four brothers and two sisters would eventually take over the family business, which was one of the biggest laundries in New England. One of our accounts was the Newport, Rhode Island Navy Base. I spent many nights folding sheets and pressing uniforms.

My mom's name is Theresa, like the saint, but she went by Tess. She was of Remy descent. Mom was always the rock in our family. She would run the show. I can remember many times when she would bring us swimming and she could do a mean flip. One day I was on my float and the tide carried me out too far and I was separated from my float and she had to swim out and save me. Still to this day my mom is hard to keep up with. Mom continues to encourage me all the time with her love and support. She had a brother that drowned at the beach at an early age and they blamed it on cramps from swimming too soon after eating. That scene was brought up every time we wanted to swim after eating. She also had a brother who was a jet pilot in the Air Force. He crashed his jet one day on maneuvers in New Mexico. He was never found. Many of my relatives say I resemble his physical appearance.

My dad was a character. Everyone called him Chief. We lived in Ocean Grove,

Massachusetts where I grew up the first few years. Ocean Grove did not have a whole lot to claim. The biggest thing we had was The Bluffs, which was where we went swimming. My Mom's brother, Arthur, owned the Bluffs Amusement section. I called him my rich uncle. He was an albino. I could go over there all day and play on the rides for free. Back then he was, of course, my favorite uncle.

My sister, Elise, was born in 1953. I was born Alan Phillip Paquette in 1954 in Fall River, Massachusetts and two years after that, my brother Marc was born. When I was born, I had a few strikes against me. I was born tongue-tied and with a nervous condition called Tourette's syndrome and I was shorter than everyone else. In the fifties and sixties, people did not know what Tourette's was or how to diagnose it. In fact, I did not know what it was until I was an adult. When I would blink my eyes and make noises and grunt, they thought I was showing off. It is hard enough being a young kid without having those nervous conditions.

My dad would take me out in his laundry truck. He always drove International Harvester step vans. We would go house to house and to three story tenements to pick up and deliver laundry. I would carry huge bags of laundry, usually wet, up and down stairs and all over, which gave me large thigh muscles and tremendous arm strength long before anyone else my age. I would work with him on weekends and during the summer. Every night he would go to the bar, without my Mom knowing. Even when I was very young, he would go in the bar and do his thing and I would sit in the truck and wait for him. He would give me a handful of quarters and I would get an orange soda and chips. I always bought comic books and Mad Magazines. I had more comic books than anyone else on my block.

Sitting in the laundry truck in downtown Fall River, I remember the people who would come by and talk with me. These ladies, I guess they were prostitutes would just be sitting in the truck talking to me and ruffling my hair and then the bums would come over to flirt with the ladies. That was also about the same time I saw motorcycle people for the first time. There were several biker clubs in the area. Sometimes a guy on a motorcycle would come over to see what I was doing. I spent a lot of nights talking to these street people.

When I was ten years old, I used to hang out on an overpass to engage in my favorite pastime of dropping rocks on passing vehicles. I had to know exactly the right moment to drop the projectile so that it would hit a car when it was right below me. What a way to learn about Isaac Newton's Second Law of Motion. Once I dropped a cinderblock through the windshield of a semi truck. Wow, what an idiot I was. One night, I was dropping things as usual and I heard some thunder. The sky was clear, though, with no sign of rain. The thunder became constant and I realized it was an oncoming vehicle. I readied a rock I had been saving for a special occasion. The rumble became louder and it was not just one vehicle, but a whole pack of about one hundred guys on motorcycles, and they all had long hair and tattoos. What struck me most was that they were all wearing leather vests and had patches on the back. I was so impressed by this. After they all had passed, I realized that the rock was still in my hand. I really wanted to be in a club like that. Those guys demanded so much fear and respect. Once a year they would gather at a Catholic place called La Salette Shrine in Attleboro to get their bikes blessed. One year I walked around the parking lot when all the bike clubs were there. There must have been a thousand of them. When that Priest got up in front of the crowd to give the blessing, you could hear a pin drop it was so quiet. I was amazed with how much the bikers respected the priest and what authority he had. I remember thinking, "Now that's the man with the power."

I was raised in a normal family. I had to go to church every Sunday, which I did not like because I could not understand what the service was about because it was in Latin. Back then, as a young kid, church was boring enough without being in a language I did not know. The antsy feeling of wanting to leave was so palpable that I could not sit still. I went to St. Michaels Catholic School for nine years. I started to think soap was a food group because of how much of it I ate. And I got plenty of ruler smacks on my hands. Most of them I deserved. I was caught once with a Mad Magazine in my lesson book.

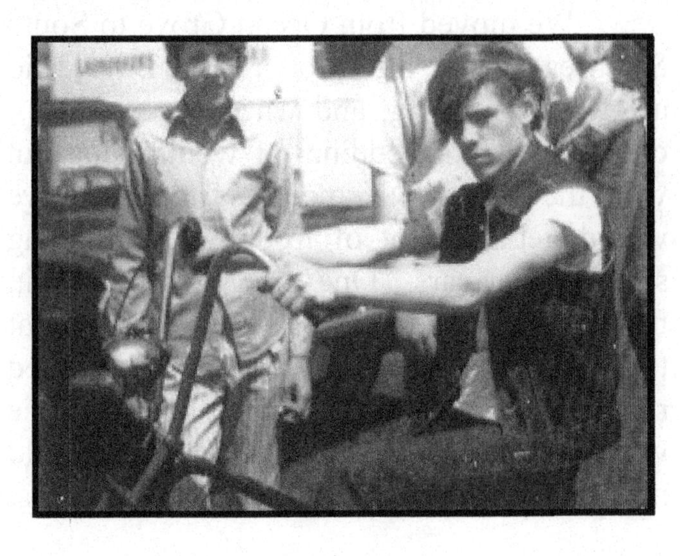

IN HIS WIND

I was always destructive. Even at a young age, I was destructive. One time my father disciplined me with a belt to my backside. Later that day I took all the belts he owned and placed them in the barrel and burnt them. I used to put firecrackers in caterpillar nests. I liked to set fires. Many times, I liked to be by myself because people would make fun of my Tourette's and how I would stutter and tic. Therefore, if I was by myself, nobody made fun of me. Also, I could escape from the cops more easily. When I was eleven years old, my mom would give me some money to go out and get lunch and I would get a muffin, a Mountain Dew and a pack of cigarettes. That is when I started smoking cigarettes and that is when I started hanging out with the wrong crowd.

We moved from Ocean Grove to South Swansea right next to Mount Hope Bay. I did a lot of swimming, and when it was cold, I did a lot of bobsledding. I would hang out with the kids in the neighborhood and we would get in a lot of trouble for throwing snowballs at cars. One time I put a rock in the middle of the snowball and I threw it at the window of a police cruiser. It smashed right in the officer's face after breaking the window. Boy was he mad. The police could never catch me. I was always the fastest runner and I could outrun anybody. We had all these forts around town: underground forts, tree forts, and above ground forts. We would steal lumber and build forts so we could hide out.

For a Halloween prank, I released a horse and chased it all the way down to Lees River. It swam all the way across the river, and when the horse got to the other side, it walked around in a little circle looking confused and it died. It just fell over dead. I guess it had a heart attack. Another Halloween, about one o'clock in the morning, we stacked stolen newspapers in the street making a wall about 20 feet high and poured gasoline over it and when a car came we lit it on fire and the car smashed right through the flaming pile, leaving a flaming trail for a block. Smart move! At about age twelve we were stealing eight track tape players out of cars. If anybody left keys in the car, we would steal the car. We would drive it around, tear it up, and dump it on the other side of town. Just for kicks.

Once there was a house being built up the street from where I lived. My friends and I went over there at night and broke all the windows that had just been installed. When they put new windows in, we broke them again. We did this seven times. They finally put an armed guard at the place. Therefore, just to embarrass him, when he was out front guarding the place, I stole a keg of nails from out back. That was just normal stuff. We ran around the woods acting like animals and setting stuff on fire and just getting into a lot of trouble. My parents worked most of the time so I was pretty much on my own.

Every year on July 4th, our neighborhood would have a bonfire. They would gather all the materials for weeks ahead to make a large fire for a celebration. One year I knew I was going to be in Canada and that I would miss the festival so I lit the bonfire the week before. The neighbors were pretty upset with me for a while over that one.

My parents tried to find a creative outlet for my rage so they got me a drum set. I took lessons for about a year and started a rock and roll band. We played different gigs. It was not bad: four guys making twenty-five bucks each at 14-years-old. Back in the late sixties, that was not bad at all. Even the ugliest guy playing drums looked good. We would have all the girls in front of our band, and we had a good time. As usual, I had to take it to the next level so one day I set my drums up on the flatbed trailer and my buddy, Donny, pulled it about five miles down the road with his small tractor and I beat on those drums all the way down the road making a terrible racket.

That year, we decided to organize the chaos so we started a gang called Pure Hell. Our "colors," or symbol, was a great big swastika on the back of our vests. Normal activities included going out and stealing watermelons, golf carts, breaking into houses, and I used to like breaking streetlights. One night I had a great idea for making money. We all started breaking many windows and breaking streetlights. The cops came down

on us, which was part of the plan. The police had one car and they were trying to fit seven teenagers in that car. When I went in the back seat, I grabbed the shotgun in the front seat and went out the other door. The next day we sold it for five dollars to some older guys and bought cigarettes with it. That is why I was the gang leader. I had the good ideas. We would go out and siphon gas and stuff like that. That is when I started going crazy.

2

You know you are truly Scooter Trash if
you still smoke non-filtered cigarettes
Aug 5, Scooter Trash Calendar

Every year my family would go on vacation, and usually we would go to Canada to visit relatives. I used to like it because I could get firecrackers cheap, which gave me another moneymaking idea. I was quite the entrepreneur back then in the sixties. I would buy packs of firecrackers two for a nickel in Canada and I would fill a pillowcase with them and pretend I was sleeping on it going over the border. Back home I sold them for a dollar each. Pretty good huh? One time we were in a state park walking along a mountain path and I took the railing down from a dangerous area on the pathway. I lied to the park ranger and my parents about it. I seemed to cause havoc even on vacation.

I continued to get into a lot of trouble in school. I had a bad habit that when anyone, even a teacher, would lay a hand on me, I would retaliate. I got in a lot of trouble skipping school and doing a lot of crazy stuff, hanging out with the older crowd. In fact, the guidance counselor advised my mom that I should leave high school after I had an altercation with the principal. I had gotten in trouble for hitting somebody or something and he had brought me down to the principal's office. He said he was going to discipline me and I told him what he could do with that yardstick. Later that day I went around behind the school and took his hubcaps off and removed all the lug nuts, put the hubcaps back on and waited for him out front of the school to look at him when the wheels fell off. I achieved my goal with him being very angry.

At sixteen, I was kicked out of school halfway through the 10th grade because I was getting in too much trouble to stay in school. I was hanging out one day with our gang and one guy brought some LSD. We ate it, we started tripping, and that is what I liked. Tripping. We jumped in my car and I started driving, tripping out of my mind. That is when I fell in love with LSD. We used to have to steal stuff to buy more drugs. I started smoking and selling pot. We would do anything: mescaline, heroin, marijuana, opium, THC. We broke into a drug store one time to steal drugs. We were eating the drugs to see what they did. Then we broke into a car and stole cigarettes out of the car.

I have been to jail for public drinking, for fighting, for being out after curfew and for stealing. On one occasion, we were at a mall in Warwick, RI and we were running around going wild. We got into trouble for knocking these women down and then running up the escalator the wrong way. The police were outside waiting for us. There were seven of us and they cut us off. I always had a wise mouth, and the police said, "One more word, and you're going to jail." I said something about his mother, I was arrested, and the officer was true to his word. I guess you could say that did not teach me anything. While in jail I took a bunch of toilet paper and set the jail on fire. My mom and dad had to come and get me out, but I had to leave my denim vest with my gang colors behind because my dad did not want me in a gang.

We used to have many gang fights here and there. There were many street gangs in Fall River. Gangs were made up from guys in their area. Our gang had people from different areas. One time we went up behind the school, hanging out and smoking pot. The maintenance man started yelling at us to get out of there. We waited for him to leave, came back, and broke every window in the school. Another time a neighbor got me mad. I was cutting through his yard and he started yelling at me. When he slept that night, I painted a big blue swastika on his house. That became my signature.

I can remember some crazy things I did while tripping on LSD, especially while driving. Once my radiator was leaking in my '57 Chevy, so I got mad at it and I parked it in my front yard, took a hatchet and I chopped it in little pieces right there in the yard. Believe me; I still have no idea why I did that! When my dad came home, he asked me where my car was and I told him it was that pile of metal in the yard. Boy was he mad. Then I had a '52 Mercury that I traded the front fiberglass of the '57 Chevy for and I blew that up racing and got twenty-five dollars for it. One time I was lying on the hood of a car going 80 mph. I would always take a dare. Then I met my friend, Dickie. He helped convert me from being a hippie to a greaser. I started greasing my hair back. That is when I bought my 1966 GTO that I liked to drag race. What a car that was! A white convertible. It was incredible! The first night I had it I blew it up racing. Then I blew the transmission up a week later. I fixed that problem and then I painted flaming skulls on the hood and I had a devil painted on both sides. I had two pet mice and one big white rat as pets and they lived in the car. They were also a good security system. Too bad I was not smart enough to bring them in when the cold weather hit because I found them frozen under the seat.

LSD made me brave. It made me want to fight. It made me violent. The rest of our gang made me their leader. I used to have to go to Fall River to buy drugs. Going to the bad part of town made me feel invincible, so we would go there exactly for that reason: To find trouble.

My gang and I were hanging out at an outdoor movie theater when two carloads of guys from a serious motorcycle club showed up. There were only six of us and ten of them.

"Can I get a light?" said one of the members of the club. One of my guys lit his cigarette.

My guy thought he deserved a drink for the light so he snatched a beer from one of the motorcycle club members. Bad move. Then another one of my guys said, "Whoa, they got a shotgun in the back seat!"

I was on LSD and could feel courage and adrenaline running through my whole body. The smell of leather, engine grease, and testosterone surrounded us. Some of my guys were nervous and that made me braver.

The vice president of their club took the shotgun and said, "I ain't afraid to use it either."

I said, "Yeah, well you're an idiot."

He cracked it open to check the chambers. I think he just wanted me to know that it was loaded. I did not care. Next thing I knew, I had the shotgun pressed to my face, one chamber on my upper lip and the other on my cheekbone. I pushed my head back against the barrels; I wanted the barrel imprints to be permanent.

He said, "Not so smart now, eh smart mouth?" and he pulled a hammer back.

The bikers laughed menacingly.

I laughed right back and bluffed, "I have a case of hand grenades in the trunk and I ain't afraid to blow all of your asses up."

There was some yelling back and forth between the bikers and my gang, so I backed away from the gun and started toward the trunk, hoping they would not call the bluff. They believed me then and backed off. When I was on LSD, I was crazy and very convincing.

The next day, I was riding down the street in Fall River and the biker gang surrounded me. They had doubled the people this time. The president of the club walked up to my car window. He said "I heard you gave my boys a hard time last night".

I said, "They were the ones that started the trouble so I finished it."

He asked, "Do you really have a case of hand grenades in your trunk?"

"What do you think?" I said laughing.

The man nodded and gave his beard a quick stroke as he turned to the vice president who had the shotgun to my face the night before and he slapped him for backing down from me. He then invited me to join the club when I was old enough.

I was always smaller than most of the guys so I was an easy target to be picked on. I was tired of getting beat up and one day Dickie gave me some good advice. He told me that when I was in a fight and I thought I was going to lose to just pull out a knife and stick that person in the butt or leg. This would not kill him but he would remember you. After that, I always carried an ice pick and one day when I was getting beat up by two guys, I screamed and stuck one of the guys in the leg. It is amazing how fast I got my reputation of someone not to pick on.

One of my first real jobs was when I was sixteen and worked at Howard Johnson washing dishes. I made a whopping $1.60 per hour. At the end of our shift, Donnie and I would steal ice cream, sit by the side of the road, and eat it, just because we could. I quit Howard Johnson to work at an anodizing company. An anodizing company is where you take these big metal pieces and dip them in the big acid baths, like your carpet moldings and your big sheet metals that you see on the outside of buildings. I used to do all sorts of drugs over there. Can you imagine us spending our entire shift tripping on acid and being in charge of loading the metal on the racks to dip in the acid baths? One night the red neck shop supervisor finally got to me and I slipped a hit of acid in his coffee. After about a half hour, he was tripping his brains out and they had to drive him home. He did not mess with us after that. Later, I got a job at Firestone. I learned how to do brake jobs and change tires and eventually I became a front-end mechanic.

We also used to buy kilos of pot and break it up. A kilo is just over two pounds. We would break it up and sell it. Then we would buy a hundred hits of acid and we would sell it for enough to pay for it and have enough for us to eat. I remember one week, me and this other guy ate a hundred in one week. I used to eat hundreds and hundreds of them. I probably ate a thousand hits all together.

I would have to say that I treated girls with little respect. The only reason I would date someone is for sex. When I was high on LSD, it did not matter where I would have sex. I can remember one time I was in the back of a station wagon and the rest of the guys were in the front and I was having sex with my date. One time there were about ten of us and we took a girl out in the woods and had our way with her against her will. The drugs would always override my common sense.

Through all that stuff, we were still breaking into houses and getting in a lot of trouble. We were illegally drag racing also.

When I was drag racing, I met a guy from Fall River. He told me about the National Guard. I could work in the motor pool. That sounded great to me, so in December 1971 I joined the National Guard. The Viet Nam War was very heavy and the next year, February 1972, my draft lottery was number three, so I was not called to the war because I was already enlisted. That was a good choice when I joined the National Guard.

I actually went away in April of '72 to Fort Dix, New Jersey. I thought I was on top of the world. I was happy with long hair and a big mustache. I got off that bus and the first thing I heard was a psychopath drill sergeant say that if I did not remove that mustache he would rip it off my face. I beelined for the barbershop and it came off. That was going to be the four months that changed my life. It really made me appreciate civilian life and I did very well in the Army. I was eighteen when I was on active duty. I had been smoking cigarettes since I was eleven, and I was still smoking about a pack a day, but it was my physical ability that saved me. While I was in Army training, I did the best I could and I earned many awards. Everybody told me how good I was. I told them that it was not that I was good, but more that, I was scared. I wanted to get it done right the first time and get home.

I finally got a leave out of boot camp towards the seventh week so me and the guys

from my platoon went to the Salvation Army in Philadelphia to go to a dance. We would hitchhike around. One time I was on leave and I wanted to go back home to Massachusetts. I flew to Providence, RI and instead of waiting to take a bus, I saw someone I knew who would bring me home. I knew that he was a homosexual but I wanted to get back home quick. I accepted a ride with him and when we arrived in my hometown, I told him to let me out and he came on to me sexually. I put my knife to his throat. He was nervous and hesitated so I cut him and left the car. I never knew how bad he was cut but I did not care.

I only had one tattoo back then. I had a picture of a gal in a red bikini with "MOM" above her that I got at Buddy Mott Tattoos in Newport, Rhode Island. Many guys were getting them, but I did not get any more while I was on active duty. The bare legs of my tattoo would stick out under my short sleeve tee shirt and the guys would want to see the rest of the tattoo so I charged them fifty cents or a pack of cigarettes to see the rest of the lady. I had the ability to walk around on my hands for long distances. My drill sergeant would make money betting on me walking on my hands and foot racing people. I had a foot race one time with one of the fastest guy who came out of a high school in New Jersey, and I beat him by two car lengths, sat down, and smoked a cigarette. We would hike ten or fifteen miles and while everyone else was resting, I would smoke a cigarette. Back then, I was only 130 pounds. I just excelled in everything that I did. When I came out of boot camp, I came in first at Pro Park, which was a bunch of individual tests. When I was in AIT (Advanced Individual Training), I came in first in our battalion out of 1,800 guys for the physical testing. I was kind of proud of that because my mom had to get me out of jail and watched me get drunk for so many years, and that day at Fort Dix, she saw me really accomplish something in my life. I really think that was a big turning point in my life. One of my old girlfriends got pregnant and the other got married while I was gone.

Once I went to boot camp I realized that the guys in my gang stopped writing me, and my family is who stayed by me. I really realized how weak the gang life was.

3

You know you are truly Scooter Trash if
you used your teeth to open a bottle.
May 9, Scooter Trash Calendar

In 1972, my mom asked me if I wanted to move to Florida. We used to vacation there a lot and we fell in love with the state. I said, “Yep, that sounds good to me!” So, the next year we moved to Orlando, Florida. I actually worked construction and maintenance right where I lived at the apartment complex. Of course, the first thing I did was buy a 1972 Sportster with a Springer front end from Puckett’s Motorcycle Shop. It was fast with lots of chrome. Then I went out looking for drugs. Up to that point in my life, all I wanted to do was get high. When I moved to Florida, my intention was to save some money, buy a motorcycle, take off to California, and join a motorcycle club.

That would fulfill my dream. However, God had a different plan.

One night I was out looking for drugs, and I saw Sharon. She was so beautiful. I asked my friend who she was. I was kind of expecting her to have a boyfriend. However, I found out that she had just broken up with one, so I kind of stepped right in and we started hanging out. That first night we talked and hit it off right away. She later told me that with my thick Mass. accent she could not understand much I had to say. I was dropping her off at her house one night when I saw that her old boyfriend was waiting down the road.

Sharon said, "He's waiting for you to leave so he can yell at me."

What a coward, I thought.

"Go on inside," I said, "I'll take care of him."

I walked over to his car, jerked the door open, and told him to get out. He was too afraid of me to fight, which probably saved him a lot of pain. I told him that he was officially out of her life. Sharon and I have been together ever since. Inseparable. We would get on the bike, pop wheelies at one hundred miles per hour and we would go everywhere. We spent a lot of time riding to Daytona and all over Florida. It was so great. I loved her so much and still do. We were and still are best friends.

I can remember Sharon and me staying out late many nights and then when I would bring her home her mom was waiting up. I thought her mom was waiting for us but I later found out that she was just a night owl. Sharon would go on to bed and I would stay up and talk to her mom into the wee hours. I would say that she was the first genuine Christian I had ever met. She would tell me about Jesus and the Bible and I would listen. She planted the first seed in me. Once I placed my beer bottle on her Bible and she let me know, very quickly, that it was the wrong move. To this day, I cannot place anything on my Bible. She taught me how to have respect for God. We have been very close friends ever since. She is my buddy.

Sharon and I got married on June 7th 1974. I was twenty years old and she was nineteen. The pastor who performed the ceremony told me not to drink before the wedding so I smoked a lot of pot all that morning. Boy was Sharon pissed at me. After the reception, someone gave me a bag of

weed, a pipe and a case of beer. We drove to St. Augustine for our honeymoon. I got stoned, drunk, and passed out before consummating the marriage.

For the next eleven years of our marriage, I was drinking and doing drugs. Sharon did not enjoy getting high so she stopped and I continued. I was doing LSD when I came down here and I was doing Methaqualone, also known as Quaaludes, and drinking a case of beer every night. Sharon told me that I had to stop all those hard drugs. Even though she helped me get off the chemical drugs, I continued to smoke pot, drink beer, and snort cocaine.

We traveled all around Florida on our motorcycle and went to Bike Week in Daytona every March. It was just the two of us. I started working for Orange County in the heavy equipment department at the landfill. Then I switched over to Firestone where I worked for the next twelve years. We lived in a little efficiency apartment for the first year.

In August 1974, just two weeks after we got married, I went to Fort Sherman, Panama with the National Guard to do jungle training. I had an interesting time. It was rugged. The first week was training and then we lived in the jungle the second week. That was the roughest time of my life, swimming across a river with sharks and barracudas all around me. We sampled some monkey meat and snake. I watched a guy bite the head off a chicken. Then he tore the chicken apart and gave the captain the heart to eat while it was still beating. I knew I was in for a rough two weeks after that. I learned survival in the jungles. There was this one redneck guy who gave everyone a hard time. He came over to us and started to yell at us and I was stoned on Panama Red Pot so I was mellow at the time. My buddy was surprised that I did not get up and kick his butt but I told him we would take care of him in the jungle. We were issued a device called a Simulator. It was equivalent to a quarter of a stick of TNT. So I taped six of them together and when we were in the jungle, I blew him up. He was carried off in the ambulance. He wasn't hurt too bad. He did not hassle anyone the rest of the time. I guess my pyromania past paid off.

When I got back, I started training for the Mr. Orlando contest. It is interesting that the one thing that almost broke up Sharon and I was the bodybuilding and not the drugs and alcohol. I would spend four hours a night at the gym working on my appearance. I was vain back then and anytime someone complemented my appearance, it was a huge ego boost.

Our son was born on June 12, 1977. We named him Shal for Sharon and Al. He was a blessing. I kept telling Sharon I wanted a pet monkey, and she said we could not have it, so we had Shal. Just kidding. We had fun with him. We brought him everywhere, played with him, and he was just a joy. I was so proud of him. He was every bit of a boy, full of energy. I actually stayed straight for the week before he was born so I would be ready to help in the delivery room.

We had our daughter Lacy March 17, 1982. As soon as she was delivered, I started crying and could not stop for three days. I could not even look at her or talk about her without getting all teary eyed. I loved her so much. Then our family was complete. Sharon would bowl on Monday nights and I would play with the kids and put them to bed. Then I would smoke pot, get drunk every night, and watch my porno. I did not do pills, but I would still drink 15-20 beers a day and smoke pot all the time. Sometimes I would drink almost a case of beer and smoke 20 joints in a day. I would get just as high as I could. For eleven years, Sharon watched me get drunk every night and I would throw up constantly. I almost killed us in a motorcycle accident one time. We went riding the motorcycle one night when I was drunk. The brakes locked up on my chopper. The bike fell on Sharon's ankle and she had to get it screwed back together. I blamed myself because I was drunk, but that didn't stop me.

There was a group of us that always rode together and we had a great time hanging out. Once a year we would ride to the Suwannee River in Mayo, Florida to camp out. We would stay up late and party around the campfire laughing our butts off and telling stories of our times together. We were all free riders (not affiliated with a motorcycle club) but close enough to feel like a brotherhood.

In April 1985, we went to the Eddie

Graham Sports Stadium to watch a Bad Man Contest. That is where you have about fifty men, two guys at a time go in, and box, kick, and karate fight each other in elimination bouts. The last guy left standing would win one thousand dollars. This loud mouth guy behind me was yelling and telling this guy how he should do it, and I asked him if he was so good, why didn't he do it. He said, "If you're so bad, why don't you do it?" Therefore, I took the challenge and went into training. I planned to be in the Bad Man Contest that was coming up in July 1985. That is how I was tricked into going to church.

I was training to fight in the bad man contest, and the guy who was training me, Bob, was a cop on the SWAT team. We would train to fight and he asked me if I wanted to meet one of the guys that I was to practice fighting. And I said yes. "Well, you have to come to church to meet him," he replied.

"Nope," I said, "I already done my nine years in Catholic school and I'd already gone to church," as if going to church was some kind of prison sentence. I knew *about* God, but I did not know Him personally. Anyway, they tricked me into going to Orlando Community Church. God knew what I needed. When I first got there, everybody greeted me. It was what they call a body life church. I describe a body life church as a group of people that are willing to help the needy people in the community. Five gallons of paint, two buckets of chicken and ten willing men. What impressed me about OCC is when someone stood up during the church service and said they needed a lawnmower and then someone else stood up saying that

they had an extra lawnmower they could have. I remember how nice the people were. John Christiansen was the pastor. I would go in there with a busted nose and black eyes from fighting trying to shock everybody with my appearance. When I walked in there they were playing seventies music, so that was comforting. It was very relaxing, and I did not dislike it. I remember little Tony. Tony has Williams Syndrome. In 1985 Tony was

sent by God to break my hard heart. Tony used to greet me and tell me how much he liked me and it was nice, but also strange. I was used to people being scared of the way I look.

At church, people used to try to talk to me, but I didn't really care about people; I just wanted to be around bikers. I can remember a guy stood up to give me a hug and I knocked him down. I asked him what he was trying to do and told him that he didn't even ride a motorcycle to back off. During the week, Sharon would ask me if I was going back, and I would say, "No, I ain't going back to church." However, something kept drawing me back. Now I realize that it was just the genuine Christian love of the people. I realized they cared more about my family than I did, so I did go back. In addition, little Tony was sitting on the steps waiting. John Flath greeted my family and me and asked me our names and information about us. I knew that John prayed for us all week long because the next Sunday when he met us he had everything about us memorized. Now that is what a real Christian church is supposed to do. They did not care how I looked.

This went on from April until July when I had the main fight. I showed up at

Eddie Graham Sports Stadium. I had been training and running a lot. I could not do cocaine because my nose was always busted up. I was not smoking cigarettes because I was running. However, I was still drinking and smoking dope. I remember being in the back room with Randy and listening to the stories about how he had beat the best guy in the Hawaiian Islands and how he kicked the karate guys' butts and he was actually duct taping his hands and feet. I remember thinking he was going to beat somebody's butt, and I was right; it was mine. He was

six inches taller than I was and had twenty pounds on me. We got in the boxing ring, and Randy and I went at it for the full three rounds. We went back and forth, and he kicked me so much that the backs of my arms were numb from trying to block his kicks. He won on points, but I put a good knot on his head. I would like to say a lot changed that night, but I sat right back down and drank three big ol' beers and nothing really happened until a few months after.

I continued to go to church, and people reached out to us. I remember people standing up, like Jack, who said he was glad that I was there. And of course, with my big head, I liked to hear that. Tony was always there waiting. There was just something about the love, that Christian love that kept me coming back. I would go to a men's breakfast once in a while just for the food and go to Bible studies for the munchies. I would get stoned before. I was still doing my drugs and looking at pornography. Then one night I went out for a ride with Jerry, a friend from church. I was stoned and drunk as usual. He asked me if I knew if I was going to Heaven.

"Oh yea, I'm going to Heaven," I said, "And I'll ride my bike down the streets of gold."

Jerry said, "Well, you can't bring your bike."

I said, "I might as well go to hell. All my friends will be there."

It was the first time that someone described hell. God used him that night. I did

not get on my knees. I just smoked another joint, and he went back home thinking that I was not listening to anything, but something happened that night. I woke up the next morning, and I had this real physical pain in my chest. I thought I was having a heart attack. I was putting my shoes on and my chest was hurting so bad. It was like God ripped Satan right out of my chest. My desire to get high and drunk was gone. Completely.

At that point, I was working at Firestone. I would roll three or four joints, my buddy would roll three or four joints, and we would smoke them all day long up in the tire rafters where the exhaust fans were. I was stoned all day, and then after work I would drink, smoke, then come home, and get really stoned and drunk. But since that morning in September 1985, I have not had a joint or a beer.

4

You know you are truly Scooter Trash if
riding is a way of life.
Aug 22, Scooter Trash Calendar

What happened? It took me two days to figure out what happened because it was so real. I was raised in a Catholic family, I had gone to nine years of Catholic school, and I knew about God and Jesus, but those were just somewhat warm, fuzzy stories. They never really applied to my life. At that point, I was 31 years old; I had been a criminal most of my life, totally addicted to drugs, alcohol, and pornography. Every day I had to look at porno and x-rated movies. And overnight something happened. I used to be prejudiced to a fault against non-bikers, straights, and certain cultures. When I was riding my motorcycle, if somebody cut me off, I would kick their car door in or do something bad to hurt them. A Harley Davidson has a little compartment under the gas tank and I used to carry ball bearings and throw them and break their windshields. Or I would throw roofing nails behind me to flatten their tires. However, that Monday morning I got up and rolled a few joints, but I did not feel like smoking them, so I left them in my garage.

I was riding my motorcycle to work and for the first time in a while, if somebody got near me on the road, I was not mad. I got to work and this peace was on me. I had no idea what it was. At work, I helped this customer, who I usually just would have ignored. The people I worked with asked me what was wrong, and I said that the 'frickin' alternator was bad. I could not cuss. Foul language was gone. What the heck was going on?

Then my buddy who I was working with, Mike, said, "Let's go up in the rafters and smoke a joint," and I told him that I did not feel like smoking.

He said, "What is wrong with you?" I had smoked daily with him for ten years.

I said, "I don't know, but I don't feel like getting high."

Then at the end of work, it was time to get a beer, and I could not drink it. On the way home, I remember my jaw being sore, and I looked in the mirror and I was smiling.

That was the first time I had smiled in many years. A real authentic smile. That was Monday. Sharon went bowling that night, and I played with the kids. We went up to McDonald's as usual to get food and came home, and I actually played with the kids and had a good time. Once I put them to bed, I went out into the garage where my pot was, and I looked at all the marijuana, but I did not feel like rolling a joint. I went out to the refrigerator to grab a beer, and I did not feel like drinking. I had no idea what was wrong with me. For sixteen years every minute I existed, every minute I breathed, I was smoking, drinking, and doing drugs. We were attending a Ray Stedman Authentic Christian Bible class. I got the book out, which I had never read. I never read a book that did not have pictures in it my entire life. It had a reference for the Bible, so I took the Bible out and I remember that I thought that it was written in Greek, so it must have been the King James Version. Therefore, I took another Bible out and it was the New International Version. Then I took 'The Book' which was written much more in my terms and I started reading and looking up the reference.

Sharon came home from bowling that night, the house did not smell like pot, I was not drunk, and she looked down and said, "You must be tripping." She started to make me follow her finger with my eyes.

"It's okay I'm not tripping."

"You're reading the Bible."

I said, "I know, and I didn't get drunk and I didn't smoke pot."

"What is wrong with you?"

I said, "I have no idea." And that night was just beautiful. I had a peace about me that I could never achieve with any drug. I woke up the next morning, Tuesday, and as I was riding my bike to work it was the first time that I heard the audible voice of God saying, "I'm going to carry the burden of you having to get high." I have not smoked a joint or drank a beer since. I know it had to be God. My life just started getting better.

I would like to say it was all positive, but it was up and down. I came home that night and it was great. About a week went by and my pastor asked me to give my testimony. As I was preparing what I would tell my church, I could not see how I could describe what had happened in my life in less than three hours. Sunday came and I stood up from my seat and as I was opening my mouth to speak the emotions of my past life came up and all I could do was cry. I remember holding my Bible up I said, "I traded my Easy

Rider Magazines in for this book." I could not stop crying. This was a good cleansing of my sins for me.

After a couple of weeks I was having withdrawals from the drugs and Sharon knew what it took, she knew the Word of God would help me. I had a choice. I could have gone back out into the garage and smoked a joint or I could have grabbed a beer, but I did not. I always said I left my pot in the garage and my beer in the refrigerator in case this Christian stuff did not work out. I did not want to get rid of it right away. I sat down and I started reading 1 Peter 4. He said the end was near, and he told me to be clear minded and self-controlled so I could pray. He told me how my friends were going to think it's weird how I am not doing the same stuff they are. When I got to 1 Peter 4:10, that's my scripture, to use whatever gifts you have to help others, faithfully administering God's grace in various forms. When I heard that word "various," I knew He had a plan for me. At first, I had to accept that He could even love me. How could he love somebody that had screwed up most of their life and destroyed a family? I had to be one of the worst husbands in the world and definitely, the worst role model as a father there was. However, I found out that He did love me.

So after I went through withdrawals and cried for an hour, that was it. I knew God changed my life. And I knew He was real, and I knew He loved me right where I was. I told God that night that I would go anywhere He wanted me to go and talk to anyone that He wanted me to talk to. I knew that I could not hang with the old crowd right now so I started hanging out with the church people. I then challenged God and told Him let's see how far you can take me.

Going to church was great. I remember going to the men's breakfast and telling everybody what happened in my life. I used to stand up in church to tell my story, and I could not understand why they were so excited. Now I realize that they saw a miracle. They saw somebody like me who did not want to change. It took something crazy like a Bad Man Contest and many years of drugs for me to come to understand that God loved me and had a very special plan for my life.

Therefore, I do believe that God allows things to happen for a purpose. Sometimes you have to hit all the way down to look up. My life changed overnight. I did not blame Sharon for not trusting me. When I went out in the garage to work on the bikes and build model trains, she would follow me out there and she could not believe that I was not smoking a joint every time. I started to spend more quality time with my kids too.

Orlando Community Church is a great church. My pastor John took me under his wing. I met with him every Wednesday morning. I started learning about my new life. All I knew at the time was how to make money. I was a steering, suspension, and alignment technician at the time, and my life was changed. The church and the singing were good, but it was not enough. In addition, I remember thinking that I never have to go back to jail and no one will ever know about my past. People wanted to hear my testimony because it was such a miracle. Therefore, some men at church asked me if I wanted to go to prison to minister. John asked me to give my testimony in Tomoka Prison, and I argued, "What kind of a testimony do I have? I have been a drunk, a drug addict, and a criminal all of my life. How is that going to help anybody?"

He said, "How long have you been straight?"

"Three months."

"You got my attention. Now get up there and tell them that."

John always knows what is best for me.

Therefore, I got up there in front of about 300 inmates and said, "These people want you to know that I had a past. I was a drug addict for sixteen years, and a drunk and hooked on pornography and a criminal all my life and now it's been three months walking with the Lord and I haven't touched a joint or a beer." Everybody started clapping and I thought, Ya know, this is the same feeling that I had when I was fighting in that Bad Man contest. They are rooting for me. I could feel that I was finally given a purpose. I knew that prison ministry was where I needed to be.

I became involved in Kairos Prison Ministry. Kairos means, "God's special time." With Kairos, we would spend an entire weekend at a prison with inmates in seminars, counseling, dealing with shame, and unforgiveness. It was a very emotional and spiritual weekend. The first step was Sharon and I had to go through our Walk to Emmaus. It is a short course on Christianity that teaches humility and how to be a servant like Christ. My first weekend volunteering for Kairos helped me as much as it helped the inmates we talked to. I realized that I would never do drugs again. I saw people who robbed drug stores, who stole cars who sold drugs, and did all the same stuff that I did. I could have wound up in prison instead of just spending a few nights in jail. God was showing me my destiny without Him. I realized that not only did God love me, but also I thought maybe He had a plan for my life if I trusted Him.

Every day I started reading the Bible, studying my Bible, and meeting with my pastor every Wednesday morning. I memorized scriptures, and we would do Bible studies together. I would drive him crazy sometimes, but John was right there by my side. He was the spiritual dad I never had. Twice a year we helped with the Kairos weekend retreat in the prison, and ten weeks prior, we would meet every Monday night and form the Body of Christ with all the teammates. My first meeting I walked in I looked around the room and here were all these straight looking guys. I rode my bike to the meeting. I was dressed in jeans, a tank top and a leather vest, with my long hair and over a hundred tattoos. I looked around the room and I said, “God, You put me in the wrong place.” However, He knew right where I needed to be. The purpose of the Body of Christ is to promote an atmosphere of unconditional love just the way Jesus wants it. He does not care how you dress or how you look. He had me hanging around with people who cared more about my family than I did and cared more about me than I did. I walked in there and nobody had tattoos. They were just citizens, straight looking people with polo shirts, slacks, loafers, and weird clothes. I remember thinking, "Well, this is where He wants me." That is exactly where I needed to be. I was involved in Kairos for the next ten years. I remember the scripture that tells us that God chose us, we did not choose Him.

In 1991, I went on a Silent Retreat in Titusville, Florida. Peter Lord put on the retreat and taught about being silent and having quiet time with God and building a personal relationship with God. That weekend was kind of weird for me, sitting there meditating. I felt like a hippie, trying to listen to God. I did not hear anything that weekend. I went home and I started getting up every night and listening to God.

When I gave my life to the Lord, I had no marijuana and no pornography, so I had to learn how to fall in love with Sharon all over again. I had to learn how to spend time with her and how to be a husband and a father instead of who I was at the time. When our kids argued, I would sit in the hall and pray for them during the night. After that Silent Retreat, I started learning many things about how to be a husband and a father. I got up every night and started spending five or ten minutes, sometimes fifteen quietly meditating. Then one night I heard a voice telling me, "Go to school." It was as plain as day and with authority. I heard it. At that point, I was working as a mechanic at a Chevy dealership. I attended a nine-week electrical class at Seminole Community College and by the end of the class; the instructor asked me if I wanted to teach the front-end class. They hired me part time at night and I started teaching Steering, Suspension, and Vibration. I was working fifty hours a week, teaching two nights a week, preaching twice a month in the jail and doing motorcycle ministry on the weekends.

I was busy, so when I heard God tell me to go to school; I thought surely He did not mean me. I was out of school twenty years with only a 9th grade education. I thought like everybody else does that I would negotiate with God. I told Him that I was pretty busy, but He knew that. I told Him that I was making good enough money that I did not need to go to college. But He knew that too. After I negotiated and argued with God almost all night, I went to church the next day and told my friend Manuel that it was kind of funny, but God told me to go to school. He got upset with me because he said if God speaks, you have to listen. So I went and got my GED then I started attending Valencia Community College two nights a week, I took a Luther Rice Seminary extension course at home. For the next fifteen years, I was busy. It took me four years to get my two-year degree and fifteen to get my four year, but I finally got my Bachelor of Arts in Religion. It was fun. I have always enjoyed physical work, but this was academic work.

Going to Valencia Community College was a trip. Here I am 35 years old going to college with kids. My first class was a speech class. I never had confidence in my speech because I was tongue-tied. I could not say mother or father. I said "mudder" and "fadder." I had to learn articulation so I could say mother and father properly. My professor told me to try not to talk like a Yankee or a gangster. Every time I would give a speech, it was usually about my testimony or something spiritual and I ended up with an A+. He told me that I was a natural speaker. On my Emmaus weekend in 1986 there was a priest who came and gave a good talk, and I told him, "You gave a really good speech. I could never do that."

He said, "Don't say that." I asked him why. He said, "Because I said that I never wanted to leave Florida, but I wound up in Africa the next year." So as you see, God ended up making me a public speaker.

God also allowed me to cultivate a passion for photography. It has added a completely new dimension to my travels and this has given me the ability to share my travels with other people. I took a photography class taught by a man named Bob who had studied under Ansel Adams. It was a blessing to be with him. He was tough and he showed me how to take pictures. For

one of our assignments he told us to take a photo that represented an emotion. The first thing I thought of was incarceration. I went to the prison and talked to the Colonel and asked him if I could take a picture of the razor wire. He said it was against the law to take a picture of the razor wire while it is on the fence, but he said to come back Monday. I came back Monday, we went out back, he had a couple of inmates take the razor wire that was in the back of the truck, and they stretched it out. I was able to take a picture looking from the inside, I later printed a photo, put the word "Security" on the front, and gave it to the Colonel and he still has it on his desk today. When the professor saw my razor wire picture, he liked it.

The college classes are what kicked it off and gave me confidence. I had to go to work full time, attend college two nights a week, and do my seminary school at night, so this routine kept me busy. I did not have time to think about my old habits. God started paving a way. First, I found out that God loved me. Then I found out that He had a plan for my life. Now I realized that He wanted to use me in ministry.

I had to pass algebra and it took me two years to finish it. That's when I stopped helping with the Kairos retreats. Jack Murphy (Murf the Surf) called and asked if I wanted to get involved in Bill Glass Prison Ministry. I told him that I had just gotten out of prison ministry and he told me that I could bring my motorcycle in and Sharon could join me, so I told him I would try it. I rode my old shovelhead up to Gainesville C.I. It was me on my bike and a racecar with a driver. When I rolled into that prison on my motorcycle, I knew that this was where God wanted me. Inmates came out to see my bike and then the ministry was able to put the program on. Like they say, before you can catch the fish, you have to chum the waters. We had to have something to get the guys out of the barracks and into the yard so they could hear the speakers. I knew that God wanted me there. So, I became involved in the Bill Glass Prison Ministry.

I was later asked to be one of the platform guests. The blessing was that Sharon was able to come with me most of the time. Shal was nine years old and Lacy was three years old when I gave my life to the Lord in 1985. They came to church with us. Shal was learning to work the soundboard. He was very talented at running the switchboards and soundboards. He has been in love with sound systems and turntables ever since. Lacy is beautiful and loved dancing and the theatre. She is just very gifted and a very special gift to us. I still remember the puppet show she did for the guys in jail about Adam & Eve when she was very young.

At the time, I was also helping with the Good News Jail Ministry and the Orange County Jail Ministry. I felt a call to be a chaplain, but now I know this was only me wanting to be a chaplain. While I was going to college, I really began to feel better about myself as a person and a father and a husband. I was feeling a little too good about myself. I kept feeling like God was opening doors, but He did not open the doors, they were closed. I kept trying to jimmy the window open and jump through. When I was teaching automotive part time at the Seminole Community College, a full time position came up, and I thought that is what He wanted me to do. They ended up hiring someone that was not working there part time and I got upset. Then there was a job opening at Tomoka Correctional Institution in Volusia County in the Horizon Building, and I thought He wanted me over there. They actually hired an ex-con and he only lasted three months, and I was upset. There was a full-time position as the youth pastor of our church, but I pretty much only wanted that for the money. God did not want me there either. It was hard at the time, doing all of that, balancing a household, a career, part-time job, two different colleges, and ministry. For fifteen years, we gave God every second, every penny we had. But, what an investment! The Bible says that if I'll draw close to God then God will draw close to me. And God was right there next to me. So all these doors that He closed, I kept asking Him, "Why?" He would say, "Go to school."

God had a plan, and when He began to reveal His plan, it was incredible. My pastor and my wife Sharon would always remind me that God had me where He wanted me. Man, I was tired of hearing that. But I waited.

5

You know you are truly Scooter Trash if you dream in chrome.
Apr 5, Scooter Trash Calendar

I was still working full-time as a mechanic and I got a call from Jack Murphy to go to Puerto Rico. My first thought was, I don't have time. I can't get time off work to go. I don't have enough money. And he wants me to bring my motorcycle over there? Are you kidding me? So I told him, sort of being cocky, "Well, if I can get the time off work, and you guys pick the bike up and ship it over there, I'll do it." I went to work and I told them that I needed about five or six days off and I needed to know in ten minutes. They came back and told me that they believed in what I was doing and they'd give me the time off. That's not what I wanted to hear. Before I got home, my bike was already off to Jacksonville, on a boat being shipped to Puerto Rico. I flew to Puerto Rico, and I had no idea what to expect. I got there and I could not talk to anybody in Spanish. But I knew that God had me there for a reason.

Philipe picked me up and he brought me to his house, and I spent the night there with them. I did not know anyone. They had bars on all the windows and they told me that this was for decoration. But I thought I was now locked in this home. We got up in the morning, and I got my bike. The twelve of us started riding across the island. It was kind of like North Carolina with palm trees. It is a beautiful island. We stopped at this one place on the way and all of us got off the bikes and went into a house where this old woman was lying on a bed and we laid hands and performed a healing service. It was intense. Then we rode all the way to Ponce on the other side of the island. We stopped half way at an ice cream shop. It was a great ride. It was awesome!

The next day we went to Las Cucharas Prison, which means "the spoons." It is a big complex with ten different jails. One is called the green monster. This is where I took my bike in first. First, they told me to take my shirt off, which I do not normally do in a prison. I brought my bike in, a Harley Full

Dresser, and the narrow metal passageways scraped the paint down both sides, but it was worth it.

I got in the elevator and went down the hallway and the prison guards were dressed in black and they looked like guerilla soldiers, and I thought, no way are they going to let me speak to the men in this prison. But I got to talk to about fifty guys at a time on five different floors, over 400 people. 380 people accepted Christ as their Lord and Savior in two hours. I would stand in front of their cell and they would ask me if I was Puerto Rican, and I would say, "No, French Canadian." The guy who was my interpreter was an ex-inmate I had led to the Lord in the Orange County Jail in Florida. He would translate for me and then he would give his testimony. Then he would look at me and I would say, "I came all the way from Florida just to tell you that God loves you, and if you want to ask Jesus into your heart, hold my hand." I would put my hands out. My hands would start to get really heavy because there would be 20 or 30 hands at a time reaching out, many wanted to be saved. They wanted a different life than the one they were living. That is still one of the best times I have had in serving the Lord.

The next day we rode across the island to Bayamon. We went to the prisons that had been converted from a retired Air Force Base. We were able to bring the bikes inside and give rides to the inmates. I ended up with a 300-pound Puerto Rican, and he gave me a big hug, a little too friendly if you know what I mean. He said, "I'm so glad I'm with you." And I thought, Oh boy. Yeah, we had a great day that day. God really made it worth it. I can still remember when I showed up at that prison, after I got off the elevator, sitting on my bike, all these guards surrounded me and hundreds and hundreds of inmates, that place was only concrete and steel, and you could smell people. I looked up and I saw a vision of Jesus Christ standing there. He looked at me and said, "I knew you'd come." Now my question has always been what if I had stayed at home. I had made every excuse to stay home. And what if in my quiet time I had heard His voice say, "Where were you?" I am so glad I went.

Everything kept getting better and better. Going to Puerto Rico was a big opening point for me. I continued ministry with Jack Murphy and Bill Glass Prison Ministry. I have been to hundreds of "prison invasions" since.

After putting Kairos behind, God started opening many big doors. People would call me up from all over the place to ask me to speak. I started writing sermons not even knowing how to do it until I went to college and learned how to write sermons properly.

6

You know you are truly Scooter Trash if you have scars to prove it.
Sep 6, Scooter Trash Calendar

One time we went on a military bike run. There were about 200 bikes on this run. During the run, there was a situation in one of the bars where this lady had a seizure. About eight of us, Christian bikers circled around her and prayed. I guess the bikers recognized what an outward expression this was for God. She wound up being fine and they recognized that God was with us on the run.

Once about 30 bikes were together in St. Augustine on a weekend for some fellowship. It was not only a beautiful ride but one of ministry also. Back then, we rode with the Christian Motorcyclist Association (CMA). It was just fun seeing about thirty of us Christian bikers just enjoying ourselves riding down A1A from Daytona to St.

Augustine. When we got there, Sharon and I went on the buggy ride and enjoyed hearing the history of St. Augustine. Our chapter president asked me to give the message at the sunrise service right there on the river. We used the gazebo by the bay, and God really blessed us with an awesome sunrise.

If you can just imagine over five hundred thousand bikes and bikers on Main Street in Daytona, that is what Bike Week is all about. We rode in on Thursday and I delivered a motivational message to kick off the event at a local church hosted by CMA. I was asked to give a sermon on Saturday. This being the main day, I was excited. There were about a hundred CMA members and friends there on that morning. God was awesome during this weekend. We had three good conversations with people who wanted to leave a motorcycle club they were members of. We were able to tell them that God called us away from the lifestyle also. You see I am confident that it is not our ability but our availability. However, God cannot use us if we are not there.

We then headed over to Daytona to attend the North Florida Confederation of Clubs. We went to a party with about 200 club members. It was a blessing to be among them. These are all the patch holders, the real motorcycle people: the real bikers. Later on that night, we headed up to Tomoka CI to do a presentation. God loves bikers and inmates. Amen.

Many of you have asked what a bike rally is. A bike rally comes in many forms. It could be a benefit run for someone who needs help financially because of a bike wreck. It could be a rally where we just have bike games that test the technical skills of the bikers, like a slow race to see who can come in last on their bike without putting their feet down. It is just fun. We are involved in the runs and the bike games.

We rode to Kissimmee to a big bike event on a Saturday with a couple of hundred bikes attending. There were vendors selling bike goods and good chow. This is no place to be on a diet. We walked around talking to people in the crowds and helped with biking games. Saturday night we went over to the local motorcycle clubhouse for their Halloween party. This was quite an experience to say the least. Sharon and I were asked to judge the costume contest. This was an honor that they would trust us, being that we are not a part of the club. Sunday morning we headed back to the bike rally where I held a service under the tent. This was my first tent revival. The Lord moved some people that day with our presence there. It was just one of the many times that I was asked to give a message. As 1 Peter 3:15 says, we should always be prepared to give the hope you have in Christ Jesus with gentleness and fear. I know that every time I go somewhere I might be asked to speak, give a bike blessing, or pray for someone. I always have to be prepared.

I spent many days that month visiting people in hospitals and in jails. I thanked God that I was able to spread the gospel in all these facilities. We would hear about a motorcycle crash and I would find out what hospital they were in and go visit them. Some of them did not have any relationship with Jesus. When I would arrive, they would hear the gospel of His healing love and they would see the love of other Christians who took the time to be with them.

Sharon and I rode over to Daytona on Sunday in the rain and 40 mph winds. It was a scary ride to say the least, but it was worth it to see all the bikes and people on Main Street. We had many opportunities to talk to the people there and to share with them the saving grace of Jesus Christ. This year I was invited to be part of the bike races at Daytona Speedway. I was there on Wednesday and Thursday before Bike Week and I worked the corners of the racetrack and helped pick up the bikes and bikers that crashed. Fortunately, there was not much action in my corner. However, Thursday about 4:00, it began to rain and I was about thirty feet away from four wrecks that happened within a half hour. Now you have to realize, these bikes are going 180 mph and they slow down to about 150 mph to make the turns. We got very busy real fast. My job was to get the wrecked bike off the track and clear the oil spill as fast as possible before I was hit. At one time, I was clearing the oil, I had a bike coming straight at me, and I had to dive out of the way. I am glad that God had his very fast angels to help me. There was one very bad wreck and the racer had been placed on the stretcher to be put in the ambulance. I told him that I was praying for him, and he just looked at me and winked. He knew that God was there for him. Thanks for all your prayers for this ministry.

We attended a prison invasion in LA. No, we did not go to California. We went to Lower Alabama, which is Marianna, Florida. This was the Bill Glass Weekend of Champions. There were 250 counselors and about 60 bikers on this weekend. We invaded 23 prisons. There were 2300 decisions made to ask Jesus into their heart. Praise the Lord!

I was so honored to be a part of this wonderful ministry. We left Thursday morning with five bikes. It took us about six hours and we arrived in Marianna at about six o'clock that night. Satan tried to prevent us from attending this weekend. The night before, Sharon got sick so I had to leave without her. However, she got to feeling better the next day, drove up, and surprised me. I tell you, there is no slowing Sharon down. There is no stopping her at all. I woke up Friday morning and found a flat tire on my bike. The Word says that Satan roars like a lion. However, he sure is stupid. Obviously, he did not know that I was a mechanic. I have a bag of tools that includes an air compressor and a plug kit. The other bikers were impressed. They timed my repair, and in six minutes, I had that bike tire fixed. It was a great weekend and I was proud to serve God in the repair business. What a great ministry Bill Glass is. We have met many good friends that come into the prisons with us, like Jessica and Scotty, who have a passion for prisons and Al and Sue, who love people just as they are. Then there is Judi. She is one dedicated lady for Jesus. Her only transportation is a motorcycle. She is usually the first one waiting to get in a prison to minister. We can always count on Judi to be upbeat and positive. On that Saturday night at the banquet, they asked me if I would stay Sunday morning and do a church service at a prison work camp. Of course, I agreed. It was an hour in the opposite direction from home and it was 34 degrees that morning. At 60 mph, it is more like 10 degrees. I did the service outside on the basketball court and God was awesome as usual. I stood there freezing and thanked everybody for their prayers for our travel. We thank God that we were able to get there and get back home safely.

The more I serve the Lord the more I understand that He has been preparing me from the beginning for ministry: The way I look, the way I behave or misbehave, the way I conduct myself and hold myself up and the way my life has turned around. I used to be a part of the problem, but now I have become a part of the solution. A long time ago, I asked my pastor, "Why did God let me do all those crazy things with the drugs and the crime?" Pastor John said, "He didn't let you, He tolerated you for a reason." I am beginning to understand what it is.

When I walk down the hallway at the 33rd Street Jail on my way to do a service, I run into several individuals who are ready to tell me their story and how God is knocking on their door. People look at me and I tend to stand out from the rest of the chaplains with my tattoos. I knock on their door and they see my long hair and I just sit there with them for an hour and talk to them, and most of them find God's grace. Many times God has opened doors. When I go to jail sometimes, I am going there for the correctional officers. They open their hearts to me and God is there to heal them. I am asked, "Why do people find God in jail?" I reply, "Isn't that where He needs to be?"

When we show up for an activity, a bike run, or a toy run, it's the right place God wants us to be because he sends people who pour their hearts out and we are able to listen to them and pray for them right there on the spot. Right there in the valley. We never know when and where God is going to send that person, but you know, God does not instruct us to witness to everybody. In 1 Peter 3:15 He says to always be prepared to give an answer to everybody who asks you for the reason for that hope that you have. The NIV says to do it with gentleness and with respect. Sometimes on our way to a destination, we may have an encounter with a person that God wants us to talk to. Look at the Good Samaritan. Sometimes going to church is in the going and not the arriving.

The message might be *on the way* there. Always be ready to stop and help someone even if it means missing church.

Sharon and I stopped using the word "unbelievable," because all things are believable with God in charge. The phrase we banned was "hanging in there." As Christians, we should not be just hanging in there; we should be pressing on with Jesus all the time! I use the illustration of the firewalkers. Have you ever seen one of them get half way through the flaming hot coals and stop to wave to the crowd? No, the trick not to get burned is to keep in motion. The more we strive to serve Jesus everyday in our lives the more we will receive His power. Every time we see something, it is just more incredible, stupendous, and wonderful.

7

You know you are truly Scooter Trash if you have duct taped a broken boot.
May 18, Scooter Trash Calendar

In 1998-1999, I had Basel Joint replacement surgery. It was a serious surgery. They took bones out of my hands and rebuilt them with tendons. I was down for two years. God just made my speaking engagements come alive. I was speaking in detention centers, jailhouses, prisons, and churches. They all wanted to hear my testimony. I finished my AA degree in December of 1999.

Just when I thought my journey could not get any better, God just blew me away. I was just trying to be faithful to what He wanted. I believed first that He loved me, second that He had a plan for my life, third that He would use me in full-time ministry. I was a mechanic for 28 years. I destroyed my hands. I worked hard. Now He is going to trust me with a full time ministry. I went to Sharon and told her that in my quiet time at night God had described to me about the ministry that He was going to give us. He showed me that I was to quit my job and trust Him for our finances. Sharon has always taken care of the money in our household because I never felt responsible enough to do that part. When I told her the news, she freaked out. Where was the money going to come from and how could we survive without my income?

I went before the elders of my church and they all knew it was time for me to go full time. A man named Jack who was a retired lawyer used to go to the jail with me. He loved going to the jail talking with the guys. Jack told me a few years back, "One day, I'll be there for you." I did not know what he meant at that time but I found out later when he wrote me a $5,000 check and it helped us to go full time. I had a friend of mine from Massachusetts who owned a furniture rent to own company help us get started. Two people who believed in what we were doing a year before, started donating to us before we knew about our ministry. How could they know when I did not even know? I told Sharon that God always came through and we just had to trust Him with this.

Al Paquette Ministries is official. Sharon and I are still on a road and we never look back. We are now in a position to trust God 100% with our finances, safety, and our schedule. We even have a ministry newsletter that I started when the ministry became official. It was kind of crude back then, but then I started adding pictures and it improved every issue that I did.

People often ask me how I ended up going full time. I tell them that God kept telling me to go to school and then when I graduated the next year, I went full time. I was volunteering so much that my job got in the way. I put God first, my wife and family second, and everything else came after. I made a promise to God when I first started my ministry that I would never give up on anybody and I would go anywhere He wanted me to go. My wife, Sharon, never gave up on me and neither did God. He took me up on that bet. He has been bringing me all over places like Puerto Rico, Dominican Republic, Mexico, and all over the United States, and it has been awesome.

It was in January of 2001 when God gave us a 501(c) 3 tax status to allow people to donate to the ministry. That was a big step. We realized then that we were not just in a bike ministry or a prison ministry, or a jail ministry. We were in a people ministry everywhere we would go.

We have been blessed with many supporters. When I quit my job and went full time in 2001, I was just like Peter when he stepped out of the boat. I had to trust God to keep me afloat. He has supplied all of our needs ever since that day.

I loved preaching. I could not get enough. I truly know that I was called to preach. On Tuesday, I would go to a prison on the third floor and go to four different pods. I would preach a 45-minute sermon, give the altar call, and go to the next one. I would go back Thursday and do the same thing on the fourth floor. I would preach on the weekend also. That went on for years. Every time I would do that, I would get stronger in my walk with Jesus. My desire to serve others would make me stronger to serve God. I could see how God was using my potentially disastrous life to help people and give them hope. My sobriety was becoming known. As I am writing this now it has been twenty four years that I have been clean, and God honors that. God honors consistency. I remember reading a marquee that said, "When your desperation factor exceeds your embarrassment factor, you're a candidate for the grace of God." I started seeing people who were embarrassed to be in jail and prison and were now ready for God's grace.

8

You know you are truly Scooter Trash if
you refer to your bike as "she".
Aug 15, Scooter Trash Calendar

In October 2001, Sharon and I went to Biketoberfest in Daytona Beach. I was on my Ultra Classic and I had the laughing Jesus painted on the front. We were on Main Street

and the gathering of motorcycles was incredible. All the local bikers and about a quarter of a million from out of state were there. Chris and Dale, a couple we had just met, invited us to stay at their house in Daytona. We took them up on the offer and we have been staying there every bike fest since. They loved us unconditionally and we really enjoy our times together. They are the Bible in action. 1 Peter 4:9 tells us to offer hospitality to one another. It was our first Biketoberfest with my new APM patch on, which opened the door to a completely new world. People just seemed to come to us and share their hurts and concerns about their lives.

We went to a bike festival in downtown Eustis. They have vendors and bike games going on all weekend. I participated in some of the bike games. I did not win, but they saw that Christian bikers could have fun too. While I was in the bike games, I would see Sharon involved in conversation with some of the guys at the picnic tables. You would have to see Sharon in action to see how God uses her to minister to guys. She does not cut them any slack. She is a straight shooter, and she has no problem telling them what they should be doing. She has a discerning eye that can see right through their soul and deal with the area in their life that they are having trouble with. In a matter of minutes, she was talking to this young guy with a drinking problem. He would not admit that he had a drinking problem, but after a few minutes, he did confess that he was drinking because his mom was dying with cancer. Sharon persuaded this guy that his mom needed him more than ever to be clean and sober. I gave him a card and he told me he would call me in the future. Another ordained moment.

One sunny Florida day I had some errands to run for our ministry in Sanford by Lake Monroe. I missed the south side exit where I had intended to go, so I went to the north side and I found out that God had already picked this out for me. He knew that I needed to be there. It was a beautiful day. I grabbed a sub and was spending some quiet time by the lake. There was an alligator in the water and, to be truthful, I was tossing breadcrumbs into the water trying to coax a bird to get close to the alligator to see if it would snap at the bird. That can only happen in Florida. I was still trying to figure out why God had picked this side of the lake when a biker couple walked over and the biker said, "Nice bike." That was all I needed. After the normal bike, tattoo, and wildlife conversation was over, he told me that he had a liver transplant and that he thanked God he was alive.

I said, "Have you really thanked God?" The man looked at me puzzled.

"Let me back up," I said, "Have you thanked God in your prayer time, quiet time, church time, or study time with the Father?"

He blushed and said, "I guess I never really thanked Him properly."

I assured him that God wants to spend some time with him and for him to get to know Him. I told him that all he had to do was just to ask Jesus into his life. I proceeded to lead him to the Lord right there at lunch. He was thankful that he could finally thank God properly. This is just one of the opportunities that I've had on my journey that the Lord has used me.

We continued to be involved with the Bill Glass Weekends. We went to the Tallahassee area. Ex-sports figures, wrestlers, cowboys, strong men, ex-military men, and many bikers shared their testimonies. These men and women tell their stories to show how God has changed their lives and they motivate the inmates to start a relationship with Jesus. We ride into the prison on bikes and make a lot of noise so the inmates will come out of their dorms. That particular weekend they brought in the original Bat Mobile from the movie. Everybody came out to see that, and we gave them the Word.

We went on the Rolling Thunder Run. That is a run to Washington DC. Bikers come from all over the country, literally every state, and show up in the Pentagon parking lot. Back in 2001, there were 600,000 strong. The Pentagon parking lot is the largest parking lot in the world. That is why it is called Rolling Thunder because it sounds like thunder when everybody cranks their bikes up. We joined hundreds of thousands of bikers in the parking lot. The bikes leave the parking lot four in a row. It took six hours to get out of there and to arrive at the Vietnam Memorial. That is the memorial wall where the names of all the men and women that have died are written. It was a very emotional time when we arrived at the wall and the men who knew someone or lost loved ones were grieving. We met new people and saw others that we know from Florida and all over the country.

On the way, back the ride was just beautiful. The country becomes alive on a bike. We have to see everything as God had intended us to see without a windshield and a metal cage around us. We could smell the fresh cut grass and feel the moisture in the air.

We saw this real dark cloud coming out of Savannah and it was not a matter of if it was going to hit us but how bad and when. We had no choice but to go south. I always surprise everyone because I don't usually get wet riding; I get a couple of drops but that's it. The time we spent putting our rain suits on was just enough time for the rainstorm to pass by, and by the time we came out of Savannah we were dry. The guys at the gas station could not believe we were dry because ten minutes before we rode it was raining so hard they could not even see the gas pumps from the station. I told him that God kept us dry.

As we crossed the Florida State line, Sharon said, "Was this trip a washout?" We traveled 2,000 miles and did not know if we touched anyone's life. Just as I was thinking this, a pickup passed us. There was this guy with a POW flag in the back. We both gave this guy a friendly wave as he passed by. About an hour later, we pulled up at the last rest stop before heading home, and guess who pulled up behind us? That biker in the truck. As we conversed with him, we found out that he was in Vietnam for two years and now he was not in good health. I asked him if he had made his peace with God yet, and he said that he didn't like going to church.

I rephrased the question, "If you stood before the pearly gates, would the key fit?"

He said, "I believe in Jesus and God and all, but I don't feel worthy."

We assured him that he was worthy. I asked him if I could bless his bike and him, and he said yes. I also asked him if he wanted to ask Jesus into his heart and he said yes. He asked Jesus into his heart right there at the rest stop in the parking lot. He said that no one had ever taken the time to ask him those questions. He knew all the right answers but he had never confessed with his mouth that Jesus is Lord.

It is just an awesome privilege to serve the Lord. He gives us stories after stories. For Him to trust us to pass on the life changing way of His Son to those He loves is something that Sharon and I take very seriously

On June 23, we went with Bill Glass Weekend of Champions and visited fourteen prisons. Sixty bikers rode into the prisons and chummed the water. It's amazing how many inmates would never enter the chapel but will come out to the yard to see the bikes. Saturday we were in Union Correctional Institution where the program was being held. Mitch, another friend, and I went down to death row. This place is a real wakeup call and shows me just how important this ministry is. As we walked down the hot, dark, hallwa, you could smell the stale stench of loneliness.

Each individual cubicle is a 6'x9' cell and has steel mesh welded from the outside. We went from cage to cage to see the faces of the men who were locked down. I approached the cell of an inmate that was huge. The guy was twice my size and had twice as many tattoos as I had. He'd been locked down for twenty five years and had been in this cell for over two years. He told me that he gets out of his cell four hours a week. He had not had a visit in over ten years. To get to his cell you had to pass through twelve locked doors. I asked him if he stood before the Pearly Gates would he have the keys to open the gate. He just looked at me and I told him that Jesus had that key. He let us pray for him to receive Jesus into his life. I was glad Mitch was there for support. He would start a sentence and I'd finish it. Jesus guided our entire conversation. Now I know why Jesus sent the disciples in twos. Thanks for being there Mitch. There were 328 men on death row. We talked to fifty and had thirty men give assurance of eternal salvation. Praise the Lord! That was a good day.

9

You know you are truly scooter trash if…
Your mailman refuses to deliver your mail.
Dec. 18 Scooter Trash Calendar

We packed up the bike and left on July 23rd for Sturgis, South Dakota to attend one of the biggest rallies in the country. We spent twenty five days on the road and traveled 6400 miles through 25 states. Not a bad little ride. Our first stop was in Savannah, Georgia. The road construction was a bit of an obstacle because they had to shave the road before they could tar it. This is not a problem if you're on four wheels, but if you're on two wheels, it gives you quite a jolt. I am convinced that there are no road workers who ride motorcycles. Surely, they would not leave the road like this. We stopped for the night after a long 500-mile day, and let me tell you, we were tired and ready to rest. However, as evangelists, our job is never done until everybody is saved. I was cleaning my bike like I usually do at the end of the day and this girl came out of her motel room and Sharon was talking to her. Then out came this huge countryman in a pair of bib overalls who looked as if he had not been out of the mountains in quite a while. It was true. He was going into town to get a double heart bypass surgery. He looked at me, I kind of looked at him, and he went back into the room. After Sharon told the girl that I was a minister, she asked if I would pray for her dad. Of course, we said yes. He came out again and he looked at me, and I looked at him, and he was probably 6 ½ feet tall. I said, "Can I pray for you?" He said, "Sure. I'd like that." Man, what a sight. Me and this big ol' country boy holding hands praying in the mountains. I prayed for his soul and for his surgery coming up. It was a great opportunity. Also, on the way to Sturgis, we drove 780 miles one day. Once you get past Sioux Falls, SD, it's another 350 miles of nothing. I stopped half way there at one of the rest stops and I put this guy's chain back on for him. God blessed us and rewarded us with an awesome sunset that night. It's just different when you're on a bike. You're in the elements and everything that's out there is able to get to you, whether its critters or weather. On Monday, we started driving to Iron Mountain. This is a serious landscape. We definitely knew we were not in flat Orlando anymore. The buffalo and elk were running around the road in open fields. Then we took country road 323, which led us to the town of Keystone. This road brought us to Mount Rushmore. Here is a good tip. If you take 323 remember to take SL244 instead of heading to the park and you can avoid 10,000 bikes. Not only that but it gives you an excellent view of Mt. Rushmore. After this Kodak moment, we rode to Needles Highway. If you have a phobia of radical turns, I would not recommend this highway. Some turns are so radical that I thought I saw my own taillights on a few of them. We rode through many manmade tunnels. Each one of them was carved out of the side of a mountain. Some passages were only eight feet wide. We had to wait for groups of bikes to go through before we could go through. I wondered how an RV would fit. Everywhere we went, though, we saw bikes and bikers. We had a wonderful time. We went down one road that was partially tarred, and guess what happens to tar at 105 degrees. Correct, it melts. It felt like we were going through mud. This road led us to a famous saloon called Moonshine Gulch Saloon, a favorite watering hole at the bottom of this tarry pit where there were about 50 hot, thirsty, and confused bikers. We had two choices. We could either go back the way we had come or go down this ten-mile dirt road. The dirt roads there are packed and hard. I looked at one guy drinking a beer and I was sipping my tea. I had a Christian fish on the back of my bike. A grizzly biker looked at me and said, "Are you a Christian?"

"Yeah, I am," I said, "Actually I'm a preacher."

"I don't talk to preachers and I don't talk to Christians."

"That's your choice," I said.

"Especially ones that towed their bikes all the way here."

I said, "Say what you like about my spiritual side, but I just rode that bike all the way here from Orlando, Florida."

He thought about that for a second and said, "Okay, I'll talk to you."

You see, there's a certain respect for someone when they ride that far.

This guy turned to me and said, "If we go down that dirt road, I don't know if you're going to fall over, but if you fall I'll pick you up and if I fall you pick me up."

I said, "It's a deal."

We went down that dirt road and neither one of us fell. It was a beautiful road. We saw a part of Sturgis that many people would not see by not going that way. Plus, we saved about forty miles. The next day we

went to Main Street, Sturgis, South Dakota. We got there early to get a parking place, which was a good plan. By 9:00 a.m. there was little room for anything or any place for another bike to park. They don't allow cars or trucks to go on Main Street during Bike Week. It's all bikes, and it's packed. At the beginning of the week, the media was concerned that only 807 vendors had shown up at this point. The year before, they had a whopping 946. You could buy just about anything imaginable that had Sturgis on it.

That is where I got my Sturgis '01' tattoo. This is like Daytona, but spread out. Of course, the scenery is much different. Main Street was much wider which allows two extra rows of bikes to park in the middle of the street. I would say that we saw about 35% of the people tow their bikes to this rally. Their polo shirts were replaced by Sturgis t-shirts, their slacks were replaced by jeans, and boots replaced their penny loafers. They hopped on their bikes and in a hundred miles, they had that biker image. They were now ready for Sturgis.

We took the scenic ride home. After riding all around there, Sharon and I decided that we wanted to see more of this area. We rode through the Badlands which made us realize just how big God really is. This place has no shade. It was a scorching 111 degrees Farenheit. We stopped in Wounded Knee where there were some Indians selling their crafts on the side of the road. This is where Custer had his last stand. From what I saw there's not much to do except make necklaces and dream catchers. We stayed in Scotts Bluff, Nebraska that night, and then in the morning we woke up to 42 degrees. What a drop in temperature! All the guys that had shipped their leathers back home were out buying new leathers that morning.

The next day we headed to Estes Park, Colorado. This town was a trip. We had to ride 12,000 feet up to arrive into town. I felt like a moose was sitting on my chest riding the motorcycle at that altitude. We saw a herd of about forty elk just lying around the town. Now if you're in a car this would be a pretty sight, but being on a bike, it's hard enough to catch your breath being in that high altitude without the stench of them.

Riding through the Rocky Mountains. What can I say? Every turn had a panoramic view that was more stupendous than the last. At 12,000 feet up the world looks different. All the cares of everyday life are put on hold to enjoy the world and the wonder of God's grace. We had a great time, but I would not want to do this on a bike that I could not depend on. There were many times that we rode a hundred miles without seeing a gas station. We actually looked for a water tower for a sign of the next town. That's how big this area was. If we were to break down between two of these desolate towns that we rode through, it would take you all day to walk to the next town and they probably wouldn't have a bike shop. The worst thing that happened on this trip was dropping my bike on Mount Mitchell. It turned out to be a blessing in disguise. When it fell over on the primary floor side, it spilled out the fluid. If this had not happened, we would not have had to stop at a Harley Davidson shop in Knoxville to check the fluid. They confirmed that the fluid was fine. We left the shop and right across the street from the shop the tire went flat from a split that it had. When Buffalo, the mechanic, was changing the tire, he noticed that the rear tire was pretty well wiped out too. The good Lord was with us all the way.

We thank all our supporters who had helped us up to this point. The blessing was that after spending twenty five days traveling 6400 miles only 3 inches apart, at the end of the trip, Sharon and I were still in love.

Now here are the top ten observations from the Sturgis trip that I saw.

1. I learned that God is even bigger than I had ever imagined.
2. He created many wonderful things that He wants us to experience for ourselves.
3. There is a different class of Harley riders today that are waiting to hear our story of what it is like to be one of the original true rebels that we call scooter trash.

4. Sturgis is a bike week that is not confined to Main Street.
5. There are dirt roads that have our names on them.
6. Laying a bike down can give you road rash in places that you don't want. Laying a bike down naked is not for me. It can give you road rash in places that you don't want scrubbed by a nurse.
7. Mount Rushmore is more spectacular than any picture we ever saw of it.
8. South Dakota has to be seen to be appreciated.
9. When you travel the back roads and you see an information sign, stop and read it. You might not see another sign until the next town.
10. After twenty five days traveling 6400 miles through twenty five different states sitting three inches apart, I realize that Sharon and I are still best friends.

10

You know you are truly Scooter Trash if you have more bros dead than alive.
May 21, Scooter Trash Calendar

I was in my 10th year taking seminary classes. Spiritual Formation class was not only exciting but was also challenging for me. Dr. Gene Pritchard was my professor at my class in Pine Hills. He put a hundred percent into every class every term. Every time I left his class, I had more ammo to create a sermon. One example is that he explained that Satan cannot read our minds. This is something that I had never thought about or even heard. God knows our every thought. But, if we don't say what we think, Satan can't use it against us. Think about that. It makes sense. We get upset and say our thoughts aloud; we tend to be out of control. On the other hand, if we pray about a situation, we are only inviting God into this thought. Pretty wild, huh? I really enjoyed those Monday night classes. I got my spiritual batteries charged. I always say that you can never get enough of the Word.

Something that I've learned about serving the Lord is always to be flexible. At the beginning of October, we received a phone call from a Christian brother in New Jersey asking me if I could perform a wedding at the Daytona Beach Biketoberfest. Of course, I was delighted to be of assistance. When I arrived in Daytona Beach on Tuesday, this couple did not show up. After several hours and many phone calls, we located them at the Halifax Hospital. This couple had been involved in a wreck the night before their wedding. As the saying goes, the show must go on. I ended up performing the wedding at the hospital while they were still in the hospital bed. They were just glad to be able to be wed on the two-year anniversary of when they met. Soon after I performed the ceremony their little friend, 6'5" and 450 pounds, walked in. He was the one who had crashed his bike into this couple. This mountain of a man came into the room crying and asking for forgiveness of which he received from this couple. It was awesome! A very spiritual event.

During Biketoberfest, I ran into a friend of mine, Jimmy, 'The Ice Cream Man From Hell.' Yes, that's his name. He travels all over attending bike events. World renowned. Very famous. I had a very good conversation with him. He told me that he had been praying the Prayer of Jabez and that prayer had changed his life. I was able to pray the Salvation Prayer with him and he accepted Christ. I told him that he might have to change his name and that the ice cream would keep better up there. Thank you, Jesus.

One beautiful Saturday, the sky was blue, the air was crisp, and the sun's rays were warm as we sat in the yard of the Hernando County Jail. Sharon and I had been invited by Chaplain Kerr to come participate in a revival at the jail. There were about twenty five bikes lined up in front of the razor wire. As the men and women came out for the morning and afternoon programs, I noticed that most of them seemed uncomfortable and apprehensive. Then the band played with the lead singer being a 17-year-old, tiny-framed girl with the voice of an angel. She sang song after song without a mistake. Her mom and a male friend were back-up singers and their praises to the Lord were awesome. During their music and a brief testimony, the bikers and the crowd loosened up. There were also skits performed by a Spanish group and they all had a message of Jesus and His salvation. I then noticed that the inmates were touched and more open to us and many came forward to receive Christ that day.

My dad, Chief, passed away December 9th, 2001 after struggling with cancer since August. We were not home twenty minutes from our Sturgis trip and we found out that my Dad was sick. Then on December 9th, he went home to be with the Lord. I had the privilege of performing his funeral on December 13th in Orlando. I say it was a privilege because this was an awesome task to talk about someone who would be missed by many, and second, because I could not have done it without the Lord. The good Lord allowed me to get through this ordeal and allow some people who never met my Dad to get to know him in a closer way. God is so great. The funeral let people see my Dad's humor, let them shed tears, and let them see Jesus. Chief was loved by many. When you met Chief, you could not help but like him. He had a way of making you happy. He was so full of energy that it rubbed off on you. He showed me how to be a people person. He allowed me to be my own person. His last words to me were, “You only go around this world once. You only go around once.” He was so right.

What is a toy run? Many people ask me what a toy run is. It’s probably the closest thing to seeing a under privileged child have a normal Christmas. These kids may have never had one before. This particular run is for the Central Florida Children’s Home. The event is planned by a local biker bar, Betty’s Laughing Horse on Goldenrod Road in Orlando. A couple of months before we have meetings to discuss what the kids want and need for Christmas. The names of every child are placed on a board with their want list. The bikers then take a list and buy all the things a kid wants. Then comes the fun part. This year there were about 150 bikes that rode to the home and we distributed the gifts to the kids. It has been a treat to watch the kids grow up over the last five years. We all enjoy watching them open their gifts from all the bikers.

One weekend we left the house at 6:15 a.m. to go to Brevard Correctional Institution. It is a 1,300-person prison near Cocoa Beach filled with youthful offenders from 14 - 24 years of age. It seems like every time we go where the youth are incarcerated it takes longer to get in. I guess it’s hard to get the correct count or something. Anyway, after finally getting the right count the inmates were let out to come into the yard to meet us. We were on our bikes on the basketball courts. They came out slowly and didn't seem to want to be bothered. Sharon said, "Come on over and meet my husband, all you tattoo freaks." And they came over. We visited for a while and then Tino Walendo got up on the high wire and gave his testimony. There were quite a few listening, but there were also these little groups talking and carrying on in the back. I tell you this because sometimes it is very frustrating being there. Not everyone wants Jesus to be Lord of their lives. At the end of Tino's talk, Eddy Gonzalez gave his talk about when he was in prison and in gangs. He talked about how he finally gave his life to the Lord, and now he wants to share his prison experience. After he did an altar call, the group that we had talked to all raised their hands along with many others. We gathered them in groups and told them that they would be chastised and what to do to start growing as Christians. The leader went by himself to talk to another volunteer and gave his life to the Lord. It was awesome to see the leader change right before our eyes. If he goes to chapel, most of them will follow and they will see a difference in the compound.

I was asked to do a follow-up Bible study in the prisons that we had previously invaded during the Weekend of Champions. I was excited about this, but I had no idea how blessed I would be when I did the Bible studies. My first Bible study was in the Orange County Jail. I was in the Capital Life Cell. That means they're going down the road for a long time with capital punishment or a life sentence. I was blessed to be able to give this format to the men in 6-B in the county jail and the Juvenile Department of Corrections, a place full of youthful offenders. I showed up not knowing what to expect, but I was prayed up and willing to let God control the two-hour study. I opened with a 20-minute video of some football players' making spectacular plays. Of course, this was about Christian football players, but as the video was playing, I realized that this was not about football; it was about the life of these kids. I told them when they saw a player making an awesome catch it was them resisting drugs. When they saw a player tackle a quarterback, it was them staying in school. When they saw a player with a Super Bowl ring on their finger it was them accepting Christ in their heart and passing on the information to their friends. I was blown away by the response from these kids. If you hear anyone who thinks he's called to preach the Word of God, send him to me. If he can entertain these forty kids for two hours, he can talk to any group. For two hours, these kids stayed quiet. As the night went on, they were more attentive to God's Word. It was awesome. At the end when I asked if they would open their hearts to Jesus, I figured I would get the normal few standing. However, thirty five out of the forty stood up to receive Jesus into the hearts. Praise the Lord! Locked up street kids aren't going to listen to just anybody. They are in trouble with a "I'm going to do it my way" attitude. You get my point. These same kids were giving themselves to God right there in front of their buddies. Just when I think I've seen it all, God blows me away with His power. He moves in people in a mighty way. If you ever want to experience God's might, let me know. I see it all the time.

Just when I thought I wasn't wearing enough hats, God opened another door for me to enter. The North Florida Confederation of Clubs is an organization, which is made up of thirty different motorcycle clubs striving for unity. At the general meeting, something happened that had to be a God thing. They were re-electing a few different positions on the board. The position for Chaplain was open and someone nominated me. God wanted me in the position, so I accepted it. I had four guys in the secular clubs tell me, "Congratulations! You're the right man for the job." These bikers would not even look at me two years ago or step foot in a church. Isn't God wonderful!

11

You know you are truly Scooter Trash if
you did wrong and nobody forgot.
Apr 27, Scooter Trash Calendar

Friday, April 12th, 1:35 p.m. I was sitting in traffic on Kirkman Road. I had just talked to five classes at Dr. Phillips High School about motorcycle awareness. I am able to speak in the high schools because I am the safety director for ABATE. (American Bikers Aiming Towards Education) It was raining. Traffic was congested. I had just checked to see if any cars were moving in the left lane when the thought came to my mind, "I better just stay in the slow lane and stay safe." That split second passed in my mind, and I heard tires locking up and felt the worst impact I had ever felt. Everything turned white. I thought, "I am dead." Then I hit the pavement. Naw, I'm sure Heaven is not as painful as this. I was stopped at a red light and a van rear-ended me. I felt angels pick me up and sit me on the right side of my bike. It's a good thing, too, because the van was going about forty mph and shoved my bike into the car in front of me. I got up, walked to the side of the road, and sat down. The driver of the van got out and was freaking out so I had to calm him down. What an impact. My bike was lying on its side and I was laying on the grass bleeding. The paramedics got there, and they ripped my pants, my good pants. They found road rash on my lower leg and a chunk scooped out of my upper leg. My boots saved my ankles, my jeans saved my legs, and my helmet saved my head. They loaded me on the ambulance and I was glad I had a chain wallet because it kept my wallet with me and my cell phone was by my side. I remember telling the paramedics about how I was blessed and I asked them where they were with the Lord. After nine hours in the emergency room, I was released with no broken bones and with five stitches in my leg. The next night I went to the prison to preach in the chapel, against the better judgment of my friends. I told Sharon that I would slow down but I would not stop. Two hundred guys showed up for the service, two men were saved, and God received the glory. It was worth limping in pain that night.

We left Orlando with the aftermath of this wreck. We knew we had to leave Orlando to go to New Orleans for the National Coalition of Motorcycles. We had been planning this trip since May. There were over forty different clubs in New Orleans. The insurance had not sent us a check for my new bike so we arrived in our truck. What a drag, but we left knowing God had plans. We soon found this out at a rest area on I-10. We talked to a couple on an old Harley. After a short conversation about how he was thankful that he was alive.

I asked him, "Are you saved?"

He said, "Yes and no."

I told him there was only one answer. I asked him if I could bless his bike. He said yes. I said a nice, quick prayer in the parking lot at the rest center. I could not leave the parking lot until I had a definite answer about his salvation. He let me pray for him and his girlfriend, and they both asked Jesus into their heart. What a blessing! Two souls in a rest area got right with God that day.

We arrived at the Radisson Hotel in New Orleans and did not know what to expect, considering all the trouble we had read about concerning the motorcycle club fights. We did know that God wanted us there. The first night we did not have any meeting to attend, so we toured the French Quarter. Let's see, how I describe Bourbon Street. A toilet. That's putting it lightly. The rest of the weekend, we attended meetings encouraging all the patch holders to be in unity throughout the world. We were also educated on biker's rights. Sharon tripped on a broken sidewalk, sprained her pectoral muscle and was in some serious pain. The bike trip home would have been unbearable for her. Gee, that is why we were in the truck. God always has a way of revealing His plan in the end.

After getting our new Harley Davidson Touring bike, Sharon and I had to try her out. We spent fifteen days on the road, traveled through fifteen different states, doing a total of 3,600 miles on a tour of New England. When you travel a distance like this, you realize that every mile is a challenge. In a square inch, you can pick up a nail. Question: How many square inches is in 3,600 miles? Answer: A bunch. I thank God at the end of each day for our safety on two wheels.

We arrived in Coble Skill, New York to help with the 18th AM JAM rally, which is the American Jamboree Rally. Although the attendance and vendor participation was down 40%, it was a major motorcycle club rally. This fact gave me an opportunity to speak to some of their members. I told one of them that Sharon and I had just ridden 1,600 miles from Florida just to support their group. When we told them that, they were very appreciative. We just helped that weekend as servants and saw our friends from a local motorcycle club from Orlando.

After New York, we rode through Vermont to New Hampshire and stayed in a cabin in Indian Head Mountain. These cabins are where my parents stayed on their honeymoon back in 1947. If you are ever out in that neck of the woods, check it out. You have to ride down the Kangmanga Highway. What an excellent touring road. Then we headed to Laconia, New Hampshire. This is where they hold their annual bike week. The country was awesome and the ride around the lake was breath taking. Then we rode to Maine. We stopped at a very good restaurant that had real seafood. I was in Heaven. I was chowing down on a pound and a half of lobster, overlooking the bay, which had two lighthouses and a couple hundred sailboats in the harbor. While in Maine, we went on to the Nubble Lighthouse, which is a good photo stop. We had to back tract a few miles but it was worth it. This is a part of history that makes Maine what it is today. This lighthouse is a landmark that shows how they guided the big ships in the old days.

After Maine, we took a tour of Massachusetts I showed Sharon where I was born and raised. I always said that I wanted to go back and show the old crowd that I was not the small, tongue tied, wimp they picked on in the 60's. I pictured riding back there with an extra sixty pounds of muscle and finding the bullies that made my life difficult and settling the score with them. When I arrived in Swansea, I realized that I was a new person and all the unforgiveness was gone. I was not the person that left back in 1973. God had transformed me into a person that can look past all the hurts and disappointments of my past. The sick Boy Scout leader that should never have been left in charge of a group of young boys and the people that influenced me into a life of crime and drugs will have to answer to God themselves.

We took the seven-mile drive to New Port, R.I. to look at the million dollar houses. It's a great ride on a bike. The weather was between 45 and 75 degrees, two hours of rain in fifteen days. Not too shabby.

We stopped at the Harley Davidson final assembly plant in York, Pennsylvania and took the tour. I was impressed to know that a couple a hundred bikes were assembled that day. I thought they were slacking off to alter supply and demand. We also stopped in Hershey, Pennsylvania. Now if you don't get your fill of chocolate in this town, it's your own fault. One town that impressed me was Bethlehem, Pennsylvania. This is the steel capital of the world. The strongest and most flexible steel has been produced in this town since 1850. I thought, Hmm. Now something else came from Bethlehem. No, not from the hills of Pennsylvania but from the hills of Jerusalem. I'm sure you know where I'm going with this. Jesus came from Bethlehem, and He's not only strong, but we find out how flexible He is, He puts up with us every day. I know He's flexible. When we get old, Sharon and I will never look back and say we wish we had gone there. Thank you, Jesus.

From time to time, I would take over for the Chaplain at the prison. I received a call from the Chaplain to see if I could substitute for him in the chapel that coming Monday morning. I told him that I could, but I had to leave the prison by 10:00 a.m. because I had to be somewhere. I arrived at the prison at 8:00 a.m., and after the control room handed me the keys I walked over to the chapel, opened the doors, and I was open for business. I figured that it was going to be a very light day, and I was not ready for the call I was about to receive. A frantic woman called wanting to talk to the Chaplain. I told her that the Chaplain wasn't there, and then it hit me, I was the Chaplain. She told me there was an emergency and that she had to talk to her husband because his brother and cousin were killed the night before. I found his name, called the control room, and had a call out for him to report to the chapel. I was going through the motions as far as following procedures, but what was I going to tell this man? I said a prayer, "Lord, this is going to have to come from You and not me." While I was waiting for him, I counseled six inmates, but my thoughts were on this man. What do I tell him? I hate breaking bad news. Ten o'clock came and no sign of this man. I had to leave to talk at Satellite Beach High School at a wellness conference. They were having guest speakers from all over the state. I was going to introduce the safety awareness program to them.

I jumped on I-95 and drove to Satellite Beach where I spoke to twelve teachers. When I was done, I jumped back on my bike and rode back to Orlando when God spoke to me, "What about that man back at the prison?" I thought, 'It's ok. I left instructions for the volunteer that was scheduled to arrive at 1:00 p.m. to handle the situation." However, God was not going to let it rest. This was something that I had to take care of myself. I got back to the prison and it was a good thing because the other volunteer did not show up. I called one of the correctional officers to personally find this man and he brought him to me in the Chaplain's office. He sat down and it was obvious that the chapel was not a familiar place for him to be. He asked me what was up, and I told him that there was a serious situation at home that involved his brother and his cousin. You could see the pain in his face already. I told him that he needed to talk to his wife and he replied that he could not because he was not allowed to use the phone. I told him that I had permission to contact her, and at that moment, he knew something was wrong. He talked to her for ten minutes. It was a painful situation. When he was done, I spent some time trying to counsel him, but to no avail. He was angry and confused and he did not want to hear it. I told him that he had two choices. If he didn't calm down, he could leave here either horizontal or vertical, whether they carried him out or not. I did pray for him. I'm not sure if he heard that day. This is an example of an average day of my life. There is a counselor and full time chaplain in every prison available for the men to talk to about losing a loved one.

Saturday, August 10, 2002 at 3:00 a.m. I was kneeling by the couch spending quiet time with God. Not praying, not singing, not reading, or talking. Just simply listening. I have done this almost every night since 1991. I get my most intimate directions from God at this time. Quiet time with my Daddy is the most important time to prepare me for the next day's activities. The word Daddy comes from the Greek work Abba. This is a Father image of God that is closer to us than any earthly father. When I spend quiet time with God I feel His presence in my life. I start to hear His voice at night and that is helpful because when I hear different voices the next day I recognize which voice is the right one to listen to for instructions. No one is stirring in the house. The room is quiet and serene. He comforts me. Psalm 46:10 says, "Be still and know I am God."

I went back to bed and woke up at 6:00 a.m. for a busy day. If I try to think about all my daily activities in one shot, I get overwhelmed. I packed up my Harley, fired her up, I left the driveway trying to keep the exhaust pipes as quiet as possible so I would not disturb Sharon and the rest of the neighbors who want to sleep on a Saturday. I was out of the driveway by 6:30 a.m. I arrived at Steve's house at 7:00 a.m. to ride to our first ministry opportunity. He set up the first gig, which was a men's breakfast at a Methodist Church in Debary. We arrived at 8:00 a.m. and we were welcomed into the parking lot by a few of the locals. We had a great pancake breakfast, and after breakfast, Steve explained to these men about what we do in the motorcycle ministry. They were fascinated by the information. Then I gave my testimony about how we should not worry about the new Christians because they are on fire for Jesus, but how we should be concerned about the 10 and 20-year veterans because they are getting complacent in their walk. Many heads dropped and as I continued to deliver this message. Their eyes did not have the confidence they had when we first came in. They expected a hard-core testimony, but they received a message from God instead. I know that God was in that room because I received a call from one of the men asking me to meet him for lunch the next week so he could explain something that God had convicted him of. He confessed to me he had been looking at the wrong web sites on his computer. He asked me how he could not be tempted to submit to this sin. I told him to turn his computer monitor towards his office door and then remove the door. It is amazing how we can avoid temptation when we know the rest of the world is watching. Then we prayed.

2:30 p.m. we saddled up and headed for the east coast to the open house for a local Motorcycle Club. There is one thing you can count on with this club. You are never going to go away hungry. They are good friends of Sharon and mine, and they were there for us when we had our motorcycle wreck where Sharon got hurt very bad.

At 6:00 p.m. on the way home, we stopped at the Central Florida Reception Center Prison so I could deliver the sermon. The power of the Holy Spirit was there, and I saw God move. There were 200 men in the room. I told them that God had a much bigger plan for them than just going to church on Sunday. I told them that God was not punishing them but rather was preparing them for something wonderful. We had over thirty men surrender to Christ that day and twenty five came forward for prayer.

12

You know you are truly Scooter Trash if
your ol' lady has defended your honor.
Oct 25, Scooter Trash Calendar

Being involved in ministry is fun. There is a half way house in Zellwood, Florida. called the Anthony House. A motorcycle club, who have their clubhouse down the street from the A.H., promoted a motorcycle run to help get school supplies for the kids before school starts. You always hear the negative side about these hard-core bikers, but you never hear the good side. The Anthony House helps men, women, and children who are homeless bridge the gap back into society. Back in 2002, Tracey and Herb were the directors of Anthony House and they worked hard to run an efficient place. They see a productive person in each person they meet. Their motto is: "Helping those who help themselves." The fun part of this run was giving the kids rides on our motorcycles. The kids were more than anxious to get rides. We met at Porkies Bar B Que over in Apopka and line up the bikes before the ride to the A.H.

I was asked by the Florida Department of Education to perform a motorcycle safety awareness program at their conference that was held in downtown Daytona Beach at the Adams Mark Hotel. We thought it was strange that they picked this time during bike week. Sharon and I went with about twenty other leathered up, tattooed, members of ABATE to the hotel. We talked to them for about an hour and told them how important this program is to have in high schools. We were able to show Florida Department of Education the eloquence motorcycle people possess and how to be courteous on the road. Our goal is to make motorcycle awareness and safety a mandatory course for high schools around Florida.

In December, we gear up for the annual toy run at the Anthony House and I still laugh when some people ask why we do toy runs every year. We pull up with a hundred motorcycles strong, and we can still hear the kids cheer over the loud bikes. That makes it an awesome time to go to the Anthony House. It is worth it. The kids enjoy Santa.

The reason why a biker plays Santa is that he does not have to put a fake beard on or pad his tummy. We show the kids what Christmas is all about. It is the season of giving. The moment we arrive, the kids line up for their bike ride. This is always a special time for them and of course for us too. There were about three times as many bikes on this run as compared to last year and that meant more bikers for the kids to choose from. Another blessing was to see the different clubs that participated in this run. It is always a blessing to see the brothers in unity helping a good cause.

Sharon and I have been a part of this run for the children's home for over five years at the Central Florida Children's Home. We have seen these kids grow up. This run is very special for us. This year we rode up with about 250 bikes strong. It is great to see the kids that we had bought gifts for unwrap them right before our eyes. Santa is always a big hit with the kids, and that year a true gentle giant played Santa. I know that God gave him an extra big heart. He did a great job passing out all the presents to the kids. I really believe that he was having as much fun as everybody else. It warms my heart when I see 250 bikers all bond together to make this celebration special for the kids. It makes me proud to be a Floridian biker.

Who says it doesn't get cold in Florida? In December, Sharon and I signed up to participate on the Day of Champions at Marion Correctional Institution. Do you think the Lord knew that it would be 17 degrees on that day? Of course He did. We left Orlando on Friday at 4:00 p.m. Let me explain what we went through to make this one hundred mile ride on the motorcycle bearable. We wore hiking socks, long johns, jeans, heating pads, leather boots, leather chaps, t-shirts, long-sleeve t-shirts, flannel shirts, leather vests, leather coats, ski masks, scarves, face shield on our helmet, and our leather heated gloves. We made it to Ocala at sunset and it was a brisk but nice ride.

We woke up at 6:00 a.m. the next day to a frozen bike with ice on the seat sitting in the parking lot. This is supposed to be Florida! It was 17 degrees! We pulled out and traveled another ten miles to the prison. I thought for sure we would be the only bikers there, but there were already nine bikers sitting in the parking lot to greet us. These are some of the hardcore bikers for Christ. The staff at the prison could not have been any nicer. Warden Don met us in the parking lot to make sure we felt welcome. The officers got us right into the compound and had hot coffee waiting for us. Chaplain Larry had everything we needed to make this day

easy for us. The Saints Band from Cocoa Beach set the pace for us with some upbeat music followed by some platform guests who told about the life-changing experience they had by surrendering their life to Jesus. The inmates were challenged to make Jesus the Lord of their life. We spent the entire day with these men, and at noon, we even ate with them in the chow hall. I had peanut butter and jelly instead of the mystery meat. In the afternoon, it warmed up to fifty degrees, but we were more warmed by the love of God. It turned out to be a pleasant day, and when all was said and done, we had 156 men make a decision for Jesus. 76 for the first time. Was it worth it? You bet! Would we do it again? In a heartbeat!

God sent an angel to visit us. She was delivered into our daughter-in-law's tummy. How else do I describe our new addition to the Paquette family. My granddaughter made her first appearance at 12:16 a.m. weighing 7 pounds 8 ounces. A perfect work of God. I always felt that God had worked extra special on this beauty. Our son Shal and his wife Tara were beaming when we entered the hospital room. The awesome part was when my Mom walked into that room I realized that there were four generations in that room. I really thank God for allowing another miracle to come into our world. Being from a Canadian background, we are not called grandfathers, we are called Peperes. It has taken me forty-nine years to achieve this title and I am proud to wear it.

Every day is an adventure with Jesus. Just when I thought I had done it all, on March 2003 I found myself on stage at the Orlando Harley Davidson in front of 225 couples leading a wedding vow renewal. There were a couple of thousand bikers witnessing this record-breaking event. Orlando Harley Davidson was entering this in the Guinness World Book of Records. They asked me if I would officiate it. The sky was black, the air was misty, bikes roared in the background, and God was present. I gave the 225 couples advice from this 29-year veteran of marriage. Do not go to bed angry. You may be up into the wee hours of the morning until you reconcile your situation, but it will be worth it the next day. I'll tell you honestly, if Sharon and I are not right, I cannot concentrate. She is my support and comfort. I may be on a mission to serve God, but she keeps me on track to my mission. Remember my priorities? God first, your honey second, and you last. That was a good day.

I was asked by a good friend of mine, Dutch, to build houses in Mexico. Now let me tell you, I am not a carpenter. I cut a board twice and it's still too short. He talked me into coming to help with the labor. Saturday morning six young adults (notice that I did not say kids), Dutch, and I were heading on a 1,300-mile one-way trip to Nava, Mexico. I did not notice any attitude the whole trip because this family is close. It was a pleasure sharing the road with them. We had this (how do I say this politely) well-used RV that Dutch owned. I was glad that I was a mechanic because we did have to stop and fix a few things along the trip.

Before we arrived in Mexico, we went to where the Alamo was in San Antonio and from there we went to Mexico through Eagle Pass. We arrived in Mexico on Sunday morning. I had heard that Monday was going to be a free day, but Monday morning I found myself in the back of a pickup truck riding to the building site. No coffee, no breakfast, no gloves, no sun block, or hat. It was over 100 degrees. What I was not ready for, was to dig these 30' x 18" trenches. Man, they told me I was going to dig a hole and I thought it was no big deal. I can do that in a couple of hours. They handed me a pick ax. That dirt was like concrete. I had a serious attitude problem and I was complaining the whole time I dug.

We walked to a church down a dirt road, and the houses that people were living in looked uninhabitable. I thought that they had a problem, but you know what? I had the problem because I was judging them. One of the funny parts was going by one of the houses and the fence was made of truck hoods and car hoods, so I guess I must have been in "da hood."

All in all I had a great time. I do a lot of little magic tricks, or illusions, and I was doing them for all the local kids. Then I got out my Spanish book and I was talking to them a little bit, telling them that God loves them. All the kids there were just wonderful. They ended up following me all over the place. One thing that I noticed was that the faces on the kids looked different from the faces on the kids in the United States. The kids in Mexico were not angry, they were not prejudiced, they were not jealous. They did not have anything. If they had a soda, they were rich. The things that distort us over here in the U.S.A. did not distort their faces. Over here, there's competition. Over there, there's unity. They all hung out together. I passed out my Harley Davidson t-shirts and I ended up giving them all away. The next day I looked and one of the moms was wearing

my t-shirt. A little boy gave it to his Mom. They have eliminated all the greed, anger, and prejudice in their life because they didn't have anything. The fact is that their faces have never been distorted by the emotions that we see here every day. Jesus tells us that we will not receive the kingdom of God until we act like a little child. Picture the doorway to Heaven about three feet tall, you have to become like a little child to enter or you have to be on your knees. These kids really made me believe it.

I had so much fun with these little kids, but the main reason that I went there was to assist a ministry. The man who is in charge of the ministry told me that I had to wear short sleeves and the women had to wear long dresses. I'm used to wearing tank tops. The guy that headed the ministry did not like me. I had planned before I left Florida to do a Bible devotion every day for the six days we were there. Every morning I got up and did a new devotion. Every night in the motel room with the kids from the United States I would do magic tricks and we would do a Bible study. I kept busy. That's what God wanted me to do. I was there to serve God, not the guy who was the head of the ministry.

And build houses we did. We built two houses, kind of little houses with a loft. But

I was honored to be able to do the devotions in the morning. I could see that the head of the ministry just didn't like the way that I looked. However, at the end after we had built the houses, he let me do the key dedication and let me give the key to the owners of the house. Those people were so proud of those little houses.

The funny part was that all the girls liked my long hair, so at the end, I took my hair out of the ponytail because they wanted to see how long my hair was, and I put it all in front of me. I looked like Cousin It on the old TV show The Addams Family, and then they took the group picture. I did not think anything of it. I did not realize how prejudice the guy in charge was until I saw the picture that came out in his newsletter and he had digitally erased my hair. I tell you what; the kids that lived in Mexico didn't have a problem.

13

You know you are truly Scooter Trash if
your wallpaper is the sky.
Aug 7, Scooter Trash Calendar

Inmate Encounter Prison Ministry held an event at Coleman Federal Prison in Coleman, Florida off Highway 301. We had brought the bikes into the yard and spoke to the inmates all day. Afterward they had a nice banquet set up for the volunteers. It was Friday February 13th 2004, and we had just left the prison. I was on my bike, a brand new Ultra Classic with only 1,500 miles on it. I had just gotten on the main road in Bushnell and had done what I always do, made a wrong turn. I turned around and came back. The traffic was rather congested. I looked up and this white Volvo had pulled right in front of us and stopped. I grabbed the front and rear brake and locked them up only to slide into the side of the car. Sharon and I hit the side of the car. All I did was break my hand and fall over, but I looked over and there Sharon was laying about fifty feet from the bike. She had landed on her hip and shattered her pelvis. I thought my life was over. I couldn't see anything good out of this situation. I was angry because Sharon was hurt. But she had this peace that came over her. She kept saying that everything was going to be all right. I wish that I could have seen it at the time. Eventually I did, but not at that time. I looked down at my bike and it was destroyed. I looked at Sharon lying there crippled and couldn't move. I stood up with my helmet in my hand ready to knock out the young kid that ruined my life. I always say that the only thing that stopped me from putting out his lights was the grace of God and the two police officers walking towards me. They put her on a gurney and in the ambulance. I knew that I had two choices. Whether to knock out that young kid and go to jail or walk on the ambulance and be there for Sharon. I walked over to the ambulance and got in.

When we started going off to the hospital, I just remember being angry. I looked over at Sharon and she was smiling and telling everybody about the grace of God. We got to the hospital and all our friends came over. We realized how many people we had that were good friends. The doctor x-rayed her and found out that she had broken seven bones in her pelvis and had internal bleeding. It was rough. We spent a total of eleven days in the hospital. The first three days I was mad. People would come up to me and tell me that God had a plan, but that didn't help any. I got angrier and angrier until someone from church called me up and asked me if I would witness to their grandfather, who was three doors down from Sharon's room. I agreed to talk to him, reluctantly.

After about three days, the anger started to go away. That's how I used to deal with things in the old days. I would be angry and then no one could get near me. I know it is hard to understand but if I stayed angry, nobody could get me mad. This is my defense mechanism. I guess I thought if everyone saw that I was already angry then they would not mess with me. However, I knew that I had to take care of Sharon. I went a few doors down to witness to our friend's grandfather and he threw me out. That was the grouchiest old man I ever met. He said, "I don't want to hear about God." I replied, "Good, I don't want to talk to you about God anyway!" And he threw me out again. I was determined not to give up on that old coot. He kept throwing me out and I kept going back into his room. They say he got right later on, but he was tough that day.

Because our friends Becky and Julie said they would care for Sharon, we came home early. She spent four months in a hospital bed in our living room, and I helped take care of her. Sharon said she couldn't believe that I had spent eleven days with her in the hospital by her bed, but I said, "You know what? We live together. We ride together. We crash together. We go home together." My whole world stopped when she was hurt.

About four months later, Sharon was out of the wheelchair and walking with a cane. Thank God for our neighbor, Barbara. She would come over and massage Sharon's feet. What a servant she was. It reminded me of Jesus washing the disciples' feet.

Sharon told me that I needed to go to Oklahoma to the National Coalition of Motorcycles. The insurance company totaled my motorcycle so I got another new one. It was the same color, black, and the same year. I had been home every day taking care of Sharon and had not been on my bike in a while. I thought that she was the best wife in the world because she would just let me take off like that. She knew that I needed to take that journey and go to the NCOM. We both knew that she was in good hands with Barbara. I remember cranking up the bike and about 640 miles and fourteen hours later at the end of the day, I was in Tuscaloosa, Alabama. What a good time that was. It was a beautiful ride. I stopped at a barbeque restaurant. You can tell when a barbeque restaurant is good. If it has a six-foot pig out front it is a good barbeque restaurant. I went inside and looked over and Scotty Pippin the basketball player was sitting there eating chicken. It was just one of those great times. I called Sharon and she was doing well. I went out and got a cross-tattooed on my left hand just to celebrate.

I fired the bike up the next morning and rode on to Oklahoma. The many different times that I have gone to the NCOM, I've met many friends. I met one friend a few years back that was a bike club member. He is a big monster of a guy. When he came to Florida, his bike had broken a piece of metal, so I took him over to a friend's house and he welded it. We became good friends, and every time I'd see him, he'd say, "Hi." When I got to Oklahoma, he was waiting for me. A few guys from different clubs greeted me and we started talking. We sat down for about a half hour before I even got to my hotel room. He just wanted to talk. When I attended the meeting the year after that I didn't see him, and one of the guys in his club said he had died two months after I had talked to him. I really felt that he was ready to see God, so I was glad that I had gone to Oklahoma to attend that meeting.

The next year Sharon joined me to go to Puerto Rico and the Dominican Republic. It was great. She got to see the ministry in action. I always say that the prisons in Puerto Rico are just like the prisons here in the U.S.A. However the Dominican Republic prisons are very sad. They have fifty guys living in a pod that is only suppose to hold twenty. They have raw sewage running down in a trench in the middle of the pod. Some prisons do not feed the inmates much. Their families have to bring them food if they want to eat something besides milk and rice or plain spaghetti noodles three meals a day. The women in prison have their children up to three years old living with them behind bars.

The country is so poor that the officers have holes in their uniforms and duct tape holding their rifles together.

People sometimes ask me if I get discouraged. Sometimes I can get distracted, I guess, like one time I watched the news and I saw that this guy had road rage, got out of the car with a gun and killed a man right there

in the parking lot. I looked at the face of the man who did it, and he was the same man I had hung out with every week, who had been singing in the choir, praising God in a Christian cell of the county jail, and reading his Bible every day. I wondered what makes a man praise God one day and the next, get out of jail and ride around with a gun waiting to hurt somebody. Yeah, it can get discouraging.

Once a year I try to go to a seminar or a retreat to get refreshed. One year I saw that Billy Graham gave training for evangelists in Asheville, North Carolina. I told Sharon that I needed to get away, and she agreed. I contacted them and it was really good because they told me that they had a scholarship for me and that they'd pay the gas and I'd have a place to stay for free. They said there would be about 500 pastors present. I got Sharon's blessings and was ready to go to The Cove. Did I mention that I have the best wife in the world?

It was a Sunday night and I was packing my motorcycle and planning to go to bed early that night so I could get an early start in the morning. As I was packing my clothes the phone rang and it was a dear friend of mine, Troll, from a motorcycle club. He asked me, "What are you doing tonight?" and his voice had trauma in it. He told me that his girlfriend's son had fallen off the hood of a car and been run over and killed. Brandon was sitting on his girl friend's car hood and she was driving. He called me as soon as it happened, so Sharon and I rushed right over to help console the family. As we drove up to the house, Sharon asked me what I was going to say. My answer was not what she expected. I told her that I did not know. Sometimes you just have to go and listen. After a few hours, I explained that I was heading out of town the next day and that when I returned I would do the service.

The next morning I got up at 6:00 a.m. and I was heading to The Cove. I thought for sure that the three days of classes and 24 hours of quiet time riding back and forth the Lord would tell me what to say when I performed the funeral. The first day I rode 525 miles to Easley, South Carolina to see our friends Dave and Debbie. The next day I rode about 75 miles to Asheville. Now I had told them ahead of time what I looked like. I figured all those pastors might be a little shocked.

When I registered for the retreat I explained to the women on the phone that I would be riding my bike there and that I do not look like your normal pastor. She said, "Oh, that's great!"

I said, "Well, *you* might think it's great."

I pulled up to the front gate, and one of the security guards said, "You must be Al."

I said, "So they warned you about me."

"Yep. The only problem is that you have to leave your bike here."

I threw him my keys and said, "That's no problem. I won't need it all weekend."

He said, "No, I was just kidding. But seriously, let me go ahead in the golf cart. I want to see the looks in their faces when you roll up." And he was pretty much right.

You should have seen the look that some of those pastors gave me. They were shocked to say the least. Some of the pastors walked up and said they had some friends that rode motorcycles, and then they walked away. Some of them sent their wives over to ask me why I was there. I said, "Tell him I'm an ordained minister," and I would give her one of my newsletters. But the next few days were awesome. I found out later how God had ordained that weekend. I can see He has really filled in the gaps now that I look back. I met many new friends like Rick from Pennsylvania. Check this out. I am from Orlando, Florida he is from Bellwood, Pennsylvania, and we met over in Asheville, North Carolina I rode to the motel, knocked on the door and Rick answered it. Rick looked something like Ozzie Nelson from Ozzie and Harriet. He is pretty straight. He told me he was from a Baptist Church and that he was one of the church leaders, and he asked me what I did. I told him that I do prison ministry.

He said, "Oh, we don't do that."

"Do you have prisons in Bellwood?"

"Well, sure."

"So why aren't you doing prison ministry?"

He thought about it. I told him that if he ever needed me to come up, I will show his church how to do prison ministry.

We hit it off. About a year later, Rick called me and asked me if I was serious about coming out to Pennsylvania he told me that he and his wife, Nancy had bought motorcycles. Sharon and I packed the Doin Time chopper in the back of the truck and drove up. Rick had three prisons, one church and a bike run for me to speak at. He even got me on the radio for his area. The folks we

met in this small town are a blessing. Rick started an outreach place called The Hope Center. The run they had was a one hundred mile ride that went through the mountains and the Amish country. Rick, Nancy and Emma always have a room reserved in their house for us and treat us like family. The hard part was leaving to go back home to the hustle and bustle of Florida. We have been back every year since. I spent three days at The Cove, attended nine classes and rode 1,200 miles on a motorcycle, which gave me 24 hours quiet time with the Lord. All I wanted was the right words to say to the family about the loss of their 17-year-old son. When I got back to Orlando, I walked into the church, which was filled with all of Brandon's classmates and many family members and friends. I approached the podium to deliver the message and looked out into the crowd who was anticipating an answer to this un-timely death. I told them that I just spent 1,200 miles on my motorcycle asking God to give me something to tell you. God spoke to me and He said that there was no answer but there was a peace through His Son, Jesus Christ. We had over thirty of his friends accept Jesus that day during the funeral. We don't always have an answer to a tragedy in our lives but we will always find peace when we know Jesus personally in our heart.

14

You know you are truly Scooter Trash if
you were refused service in a restaurant.
May 29, Scooter Trash Calendar

In May 2005, we rode to Atlanta, Georgia. It was a beautiful ride. The weather was good. I stopped at a rest area and this small toddler came running over and gave me a big hug on my leg which stopped me in my tracks. He looked up at me and smiled. I felt like it was a hug from Jesus. His dad looked at me, nodded and they just walked off. I had started my seminary degree in 1991 and to be honest I never thought the day would come when I'd be standing on a stage with over 2,000 students graduating from Luther Rice College. It's the same stage where Dr. Charles Stanley preaches every week at the First Baptist Church of Atlanta. I now officially have my Bachelor of Arts in Religion. I had gone to Valencia Community

College two nights a week for four years and I was receiving my seminary education through an extension course for fifteen years. After Sharon saw me stoned and drunk for eleven years and a total disgrace as a father and husband, she watched me get my college degree. It was one of those wonderful days where I really felt the presence of God.

We got up the next morning and rode over to Wilmington, South Carolina where we spent the night. The next morning we rode three hours to a military base in Morehead City, North Carolina to get on a ferry that would bring us to an island off the outer banks. We rode about fifteen miles across the island to take another ferry 40 minutes to Cape Hatteras. It was quite an experience to put the motorcycle on the boat. Every wave that we encountered I felt that my motorcycle was going in the water. It really put some strain on the kickstand that it was leaning on. Many people and bikers take this short cut by using the ferry traveling Virginia to North Carolina. After we spent a couple of days riding on the Outer Banks, we went on over to Nags Head. We stopped to check out a lighthouse. It has been there since 1872 so we thought what the heck, it is time to look at it. It is a good place to take a little culture in. Speaking of culture, we did eat at a very highly recommended place that also has a catchy name, Big Al's. We took the scenic state road 301 all the way down to sunny Florida. It was a wonderful time. Praise God!

I go to death row once a month at Union C.I. in Starke, Florida. Well, it is time for me to do what God has called me to do. It is about 160 miles from my house, and I ride my bike. I blast up there on the highway but I take the long way back to unwind. I have to go through fourteen doors to get all the way back to death row. Twelve of the doors I have to be buzzed in, have to be physically opened by the guards in the control room. I get over to the chapel to load a push cart with reading materials and then it's a long walk to the death row passageway. I approach a gate, push the button and when they open the door for me there is a sidewalk with fence totally enclosing it. It takes me 300 steps to approach the next door. The last 200 yards has an electric fence all the way around it. I finally get all the way back to death row and there's six, two floor corridors with men in cages. The first thing that hits you is the heat and the smell of people. I start walking down with my cart and approach the inmates. Some men are sleeping, some are working out, some are reading their Bible, and some are playing chess. There is another aisle called the suicide watch and guards walk through there once every hour to make sure everybody is still breathing. The inmates only get out for exercise twice a week for two hours at a time. They can play volleyball or basketball, and then shower in that two-hour period.

As I walk, there are many guys that don't need anything and do not want books. I will ask them how they're doing and if they respond, I will stop and talk to them and sometimes I'll sit down right in front of their cell to visit. One guy has been there over 30 years and many guys have been there over 25 years just sitting in their 6'x9' cell with their locker, toilet, sink, bunk, a TV, and a little fan, and that's it. That is their life. These men will never touch a blade of grass again. They'll always be surrounded by concrete. They'll never see a puppy dog. They'll never touch a human being. All their visits are through a glass with a phone. Even if I never get through to some of them, I still want to be there for them because they don't have much else.

One year there was a guy executed. His name was Mark. I would just say hi to Mark and befriended him every month. The prison next door has the death chamber. He was moved next door when his execution day was set. The Lord put it on my heart to write Mark. Mark had to get in touch with the hatred that the family of his victim had for him because of his violent crime. Let me put it this way; I help a lot of people live, but now God was using me to help Mark die. Mark, in his letters, did come to know the Lord. The day he was executed, the news media said that he did not have any last words. But, the day before he was executed, I got a last letter from Mark:

Thank you for your letter, but more so, thank you for being there for me and helping me so much with my spiritual walk. I can't thank you enough for that. I was certainly lost, but you helped to bring me out of the dark into the light. Thank you for helping me through all the difficult times. Thank you for being by my side, a friend, a spiritual advisor. So you asked how I'm holding up. I'm doing just fine. I'm ok and I will be ok. If my eternal journey begins July 1st know how much I have appreciated you. You're a great guy and a friend. Thanks for everything. Your friend, Mark

The next day, they put a needle in his vein and injected a lethal dose in him, and he was executed. But Mark got to know the real Jesus Christ and he's walking with Him right now.

And that's why I go to death row, for opportunities like that. Mark showed me how to die in peace, and I'm showing others how to live.

One day I was in the lockdown section of a prison and I started a conversation with a young inmate. He told me that he had just received a life sentenced and that he had nothing to live for. I told him that he could be used while he was in prison and I think I got him thinking about how he could be useful even in prison. I asked him if I could pray for him and he said yes. He reached out of his jail cell and when I went to grab his hands to pray he dropped a razor that he had been holding.

So I prayed with one eye opened. He prayed the prayer of salvation and after we were done he told me that he was going to use that razor to commit suicide that day. I felt that I was in the right place at the right time that day.

15

You know you are truly Scooter Trash if
the bouncer ask you to politely to leave.
July 9, Scooter Trash Calendar

While watching a chopper show one day I decided to build a theme bike for the guys and gals in prison. I had a gas tank lying around and my friends helped me with fenders and this and that. I built a motorcycle called 'Doin Time' and it is dedicated to all the men and women doin' time. It took me seven months to build. I used handcuffs and razor wire. I even used authentic pins from many different prisons, a night stick for a shifter, a door handle from a prison cell, and a jail house tattoo gun. I assembled it in my garage and then brought it to my friend Brian at the Motorcycle Clinic where he worked his magic. He fabricated the prison parts to become functional on the bike. I built it to encourage inmates and to let them know that there are still people that care about them out here. The Doin' Time Chopper has been quite a hit.

During Bike Week Charlie Daniels was going to play and Dave asked me if I wanted to meet him because he was doing an interview with him. I went into Charlie's RV and Dave was asking him questions for a magazine article. I never knew that Charlie Daniels had made his peace with God and was a Christian. I asked him if I could pray for him and he said yes and told everyone to be quiet. He took his hat off and bowed his head and we prayed. When we were done he looked at me and said, "Thanks. I needed that before I get on stage." As I was walking out his promoter said, "You know, you're only one of two persons that can get him to take his hat off, and the other one is a female."

We do a Biker Easter Service every year on Lake Monroe in Sanford, Florida. We have hundreds of bikers show up and a lot of them are from different motorcycle clubs. I put a cross with chicken wire wrapped around it out by the lake. After I give the message, they walk over to the cross and place flowers on the cross. By the time we are done the cross is filled with flowers. Then we have a bike blessing. It is a good time for people that have not been in church for a long time to get together and worship.

One day I was in the prison chapel and the chaplain was playing an old black and white movie. A hundred guys showed up to watch it. I knew something was wrong if they could fill up the chapel to see an old movie but only a handful of guys would come out for the chapel service. I prayed about it and I asked God for an answer. I heard the word "entertainment". They want entertainment. We had put on Christian plays before and we've seen many guys show up for them. I asked the chapel clerks, "What if we try to do a play every month?" One guy said that it would be impossible. If you tell me that something is impossible, I'm ready to take on the challenge.

David, an inmate, was to be my right hand man inside. We started brainstorming what the theatrical team was going to be called. We decided to call them Palanka Players. Palanka is a Greek word meaning "lever." When you can't lift a heavy object up you use a lever to make it easier. When we could not get the guys to come into the chapel to listen to the word of God we used a lever to attract them in.

The first thing we had to do was form a team. Therefore we made a poster saying that we needed some people that were actors and willing to help with the plays. They had to be spiritually grounded. We ended up getting about fifteen guys willing to help. Some of these guys didn't have any hope for their future, they didn't have any direction and they started telling us that this meant a lot to them. The Palanka Players performed their first play about the Good Samaritan story called "You Can't Keep a Good Man Down." I made a theatrical poster that did not look churchy. It looked like a regular poster for a play on Broadway to encourage the inmates to come to the chapel. The actors practiced seven days a week. They wrote and directed the entire play and I did the background on a big screen TV. I would do the transitions so it looked like they were in a certain place like a church or a prison yard. The theme was always a good Christian theme, but at the end of the play you would realize that the audience was actually part of the play. The audience would find themselves being involved personally with the play and at times interacting.

I would stand by the dining hall and hand out tickets to invite the inmates to come to the play. The first time we did it we had thirty guys show up. The next month seventy five people came. It continued to grow to a packed chapel. What the play did was get their emotions massaged. They would be laughing, then they'd be crying, and by the end they were ready to surrender to Christ. I get many letters telling me that the bonding among the players meant a lot to them. Just recently, I received a letter from a former Palanka Player and he had been transferred to another prison. He was so proud to tell us that he has started the Palanka Players in his chapel. The plays continue on.

We were asked to come to South Carolina by Pappy, a friend of ours we met about four years before. Pappy was a wrestler from the old days and now he is a Christian wrestler. We stayed about seventeen miles up the road in Barnwell, South Carolina. We got a good night's rest and went over to the National Guard Armory. They had a benefit for the American Cancer Society and a bike show. Pappy's crew really worked hard making the day flow by with all the entertainment. I was hanging out with the kids and making balloon animals. I had my Doin' Time Chopper on display. We were having a great time. I was talking to everybody walking by and a woman introduced herself as a warden in a local jail. Sharon asked, "What's the chance of getting in there tonight." The warden and Sharon made the arrangements for us to get in that night. We went down the road to Allendale to the local jail and I spoke there for about forty five minutes. Out of thirty eight men about four of them really made their peace with God and were saved that night. I knew something good happened because as we were getting ready to leave, the officer said, "You better get going, there's a bad storm coming." His description of a bad storm did not do it justice because it was actually a tornado.

We rode down the road and there was this eerie feeling, a strange energy in the air. There was nobody on the road and it was windy. I whipped underneath a gas station cover and our truck was lifting off the ground, the trees were blowing around, shingles were flying off, pieces of metal were going all over the place and we decided that we needed to get back to the motel. We drove down this road and the trees were falling in the road and this one guy said, "Follow me!" and he went into this guy's yard but we turned around and came back because we didn't want to get stuck down this road. There were no lights on in town, so we headed under this shelter with an overhang for protection. It was dangerous and the chopper was in the back. In about five minutes the truck radio said there were two more storms coming so we stayed right there.

With all the rain, hail and wind it was scary. However when you work for the Lord and when you're in a front line ministry like us, radical things are going to happen. It was worth it just to have those four guys make their peace with God. On the drive back to Florida we saw where the tornado tore up the area.

We packed up and put the Doin' Time Chopper in the truck and headed for Ohio. After a good night's rest in Sweetwater, Tennessee, we were on the road to Sharon's aunt's house in Fountain City, Indiana where we dropped her mom off. On Saturday, Sharon and I left for the beautiful farm land of Indiana and Ohio. On the way we stopped at a custom cycle shop and got to pray with the owner. Then we headed for our destination in Ohio. I was asked to speak in a church. I rode my bike into the church and I spoke in two services that day. They had a bike show going on and a big barbeque. We knew that we had gone up there to encourage some people because about 300 showed up.

The next day we headed over to Sandusky, Ohio where they have a bike week. Many bikers were there, so we hung around a little while and visited with some vendors that we knew from Florida. We got a souvenir in pin and headed down to Mansfield, Ohio.

The Ohio State Reformatory Prison is located here. They built it in 1885 and it was closed in 1990. In 1994, they filmed the "Shawshank Redemption." movie. You might have seen that movie. It is one of my favorite movies, so I said how cool would that be to take a picture of my prison chopper in front of one of the most famous prisons in the world. It is where they also filmed "Air Force One" and a few others. When they filmed "Shawshank Redemption" the owners of the prison said, "Do what you want with this prison. They're going to tear it down anyway." Well the Historical Society of Ohio decided that they were not going to tear it down. They made a museum out of it and they have daily tours. In fact, you can spend the entire night because

they have haunted ghost tours. However, we decided it was spooky enough during the day.

We pulled up to the entrance before any tourists showed up. We showed the lady that worked there the chopper. She freaked out and thought it was awesome. She let us go on in so we could take pictures of it in front of the prison. I knew that I had to have a piece of this prison for my bike. I talked to the maintenance man and he took me all the way down into the basement where nobody goes. He showed me a contraption that was made of brass and glass. He did not know what it was but I could see me using a brass rod from this device to place on my bike. Being polite I took the entire contraption and placed it in our truck. When I got home I read on the side cap, Westinghouse X-ray. It was the x-ray machine they invented in 1974 to use in the Vietnam war. It was the original x-ray machine they used in this prison. I took the brass rod, polished it up, drilled a couple holes and installed it on the front brake caliper of my chopper.

Later that day they had a special opening for the bike week they had going on in Sandusky. About fifty bikes rode in and saw my bike parked out front and they liked the chopper that was purpose built. That was a great moment for us.

16

You know you are truly Scooter Trash if
the chain on your wallet is rusty.
Jul 28, Scooter Trash Calendar

I get to hang out with many of the bike clubs and I consider them my friends. One day I was invited by a motorcycle club to go to Tampa from Orlando, which is about ninety miles away. There were thirteen bikes and fourteen people. One guy had his wife with him. They ride fast, they ride aggressive, and they ride safe. They ride side-by-side and very close, and I told them, "I'm too old to do that, so I'm going to stay in the back." I was the second to the last bike.

Then the unexpected happened. We were going down the road and I was taking pictures. I was on the right hand side of the pack. Ten seconds later, this car crossed over into our lane and came at us head on. It destroyed bikes, pieces of metal were flying, and people were being launched left and right. About thirty seconds later, there was a quarter mile stretch of gas and metal and plastic. One bike burst into thirteen feet of flames. I remember looking up and thinking, "Lord, I need to go to somewhere soft." I went over to the right, and the guy on the left got hit head on. He crashed into me and I dragged him about forty feet. I slid on the asphalt and the engine guard kept the bike off the ground and off my leg. I landed on the grass and later found out that I broke a rib, tore up the ligaments in my left hand and my right arm was bleeding. When I got off the ground I thought I whispered, "Praise God!" but the guy next to me said that I was yelling. I could not believe that I was still alive and had no bones hanging out.

I looked around and one guy, about 380 pounds, was all covered in blood. The guy next to me had part of his heel removed. It looked like a battle scene. I guess I passed out for about thirty seconds and when I woke up and I knew that I had to go pray for my friends. Prior to this I had taken an Accident Scene Management Class so I helped to assist any way that I could. I knew that I needed to take pictures of the site. I got some incredible pictures of the accident. I went over to one of my friends and he was yelling about his leg and his leg was completely torn off. As I got all the way down to the front of the pack I started getting weak, so I turned around and went back and dealt with the police officer and told him what happened. The driver of the car was on all these drugs and he supposedly passed out, veered into our lane and hit the bikes. All the bikes on the left side of the pack were hit head on. Three guys each eventually lost one of their legs. There have been many surgeries and life changing consequences because of those few minutes. Twelve people were injured in all the mess. Thankfully no one died.

I kept having nightmares when I got home and I asked the Lord to show me through His eyes because all I could see through my eyes was this terrible accident where people were injured. I saw where everybody had landed in the grass, and God showed me a picture where every time somebody was hit a guardian angel would come and pick that person up and lay him in the grass so that it wouldn't be any worse than it was. It was terrible, but no head injuries, nobody paralyzed, nobody dead. I told these guys that in Psalm 119 it says, "I will send my angels to bear you up." The man who hit us died a year later without ever losing his license or spending a night in jail.

IN HIS WIND

A man named Tom called me one day. He said he had seen my article in Dixie Biker, a magazine that I write for. He had a very severe form of cancer and he knew he had to make his peace with God and he had to come see me. I was still healing from the accident, so I told Tom that if he'd come to the house we could talk. So a few days later I hear a knock on the door and Tom's there saying, "I need to get my soul right."

I said, "You're at the right place."

Tom looked like just a skeleton with skin on. The cancer had completely torn him up. You could see that it had gotten the best of him. I sat with Tom for an hour. We prayed, we talked, we laughed, and Tom made his peace with God. Sharon asked his wife, how long they'd been married. She said they had been together 17 years but they were never married. Sharon explained the logistics of being married when he passes away and that she would have no rights. We set a date and we were going to make them husband and wife. In about two weeks I went up there and everybody knew it was a celebration, but also, not too much longer before Tom was going to pass away. Tom had to sit down he was so weak. I performed the wedding and we had a joyous occasion. Two weeks later,

Tom died. Tom had made his peace with God.

The reason I'm writing this book is to encourage people who are struggling. There is a certain recipe, a certain formula, that if you follow daily as I have, you can make it through this journey called life. I'm going on twenty four years of being clean and sober walking with the Lord. As I write this book it's 2009 and I've been clean since 1985. I get up in the morning, I get up in the middle of the night and I spend time with God. I study His Word. I pray to Him. I am in fellowship because I need to be able to tell people if I have problems and I need to be available to help other people out.

The biggest thing about fellowship is if you are not in fellowship, you are able to hide stuff. That includes leaders, too. If you are addicted to drugs, the day you get off drugs you need to go to church. Do not worry about the messenger; listen to the message. Do not make excuses why you should not go, just find reasons why you should go. It does not matter if you have to work on Sundays. There are churches open on Wednesday night and Saturday night. Just quit making excuses, quit blaming everybody outside yourself. It is not about you anymore. Once you do that, you become a man or woman that God destined you to be. Go to a church and listen. Then get involved in a Bible study. Get involved in ministry. That is the most important aspect of walking with the Lord, being in ministry. Get busy so you do not have time to think about your past. If you want to stop drinking, stop hanging out with drunks. If you want to quit doing drugs, quit hanging out with drug addicts. Start being part of the solution instead the problem. Start telling people that you've been clean for a day, then a week, then a year, then twenty four years like me and you will stay clean. You have been through the test, now you need to give your testimony. Every day you brag about your sobriety you get stronger in your walk. Continue to press on. When I believed that people depended on me being clean and sober I had a goal for my life.

For the churches: how do you get someone to feel welcome in your church? We should reach out to that new person walking into your church for the first time. Sometimes we get into those holy huddles. We're all guilty of that. When we have not seen our church family all week and we talk to each other, that guest, that new person, walks in and maybe is not acknowledged. People are going to church to be accepted. But you know, when people walk into church you should do what my church did. They made me feel welcomed. You greet that person. If he or she is a new person, ask that person their name, their spouse's name, their kid's names, where they work, their hobbies, and write that down when they walk away. Then do for that person what Jesus told us to do, pray for that person all week. By the end of the week, you'll have their information memorized. When they come back the next week and you remember their names or you ask about their work they will feel accepted. You will be doing what Jesus told us to do, to be a Disciple

How do you witness to a hardcore biker or someone different? Someone walks in with long hair, tattoos, and doesn't smell quite right, what do you do? Do you do like many churches and avoid them? Are you afraid of them? Do you accept them as Jesus says with unconditional love regardless of who they are and what they do? Do you love that person or do you judge them for how they dress? Do you judge the girls in skimpy outfits or pray for their souls that need the light of Jesus?

How do you get into the motorcycle ministry? Many church members call me up saying they want to put a patch on their back, get into motorcycle ministry, and don't know how. What you need to do is find out where the bike nights are, find out where the bike fests are, and hang out. When you talk to a biker, just be you. Do not be someone you are not. They know who you are. If you do not have tattoos, do not go out and get tattoos. Do not grow your hair. They do not care what you look like. They just care that you care about them. Just go over there and talk about their bike. Bikers love to show off their bikes. Talk about their bike and they'll talk about it with you. If you see two bikers off by themselves talking, don't go interrupt them, let them have their space. It's all about respect. It's all about protocol. Before you put a patch on your back, go to the local clubhouse and ask permission. Don't just put a patch on your back and start riding around on motorcycles. That would be disrespectful. You need to let them know first.

I just want to encourage everybody that God is still in the business of beating the odds. The scripture that God gave me 24 years ago, 1 Peter 4:10, "Use whatever gift you have to help others, faithfully administering God's grace in various forms," still applies. If you look around this crazy world, we are all various forms. We are all created uniquely.

IN HIS WIND

I saw the good, the bad, and the ugly Al. But now he is a new creation and I live a truly blessed life as his wife. God is still in the miracle business so do not give up. You too can reap His blessings.

In His Wind, Sharon

Photos

Get Al's humorous Scooter Trash perpetual calendar useable year after year and with a different biker saying every day.

Just 4½ X 5½ inches. It sets neatly on your desk or counter.

Available at
www.hd4jc.com

Made in the USA
Middletown, DE
03 September 2024

60237498R00106